THE CAUSES

THE CAUSES

Cathy Stonehouse

PEDLAR PRESS | ST. JOHN'S

For information, write Pedlar Press at
113 Bond Street, St. John's NL A1C 1T6 Canada

Cover Art	"24 de marzo" by Alejandro Abt, 2010, street art
Proofreader	Ken Sparling
Design	Emma Dawn Allain
Typeface	ITC New Baskerville / Mr Eaves Modern
Printed in Canada	Coach House Printing, Toronto

Library and Archives Canada Cataloguing in Publication

Title: The causes / Cathy Stonehouse.

Names: Stonehouse, Cathy, author.

Identifiers: Canadiana 20190101555 | ISBN 9781897141953 (softcover)

Classification: LCC PS8587.T674 C38 2019 | DDC C813/.54—dc23

Acknowledgments

The publisher wishes to thank the Canada Council for the Arts and the NL Publishers Assistance Program for their generous support of our publishing program.

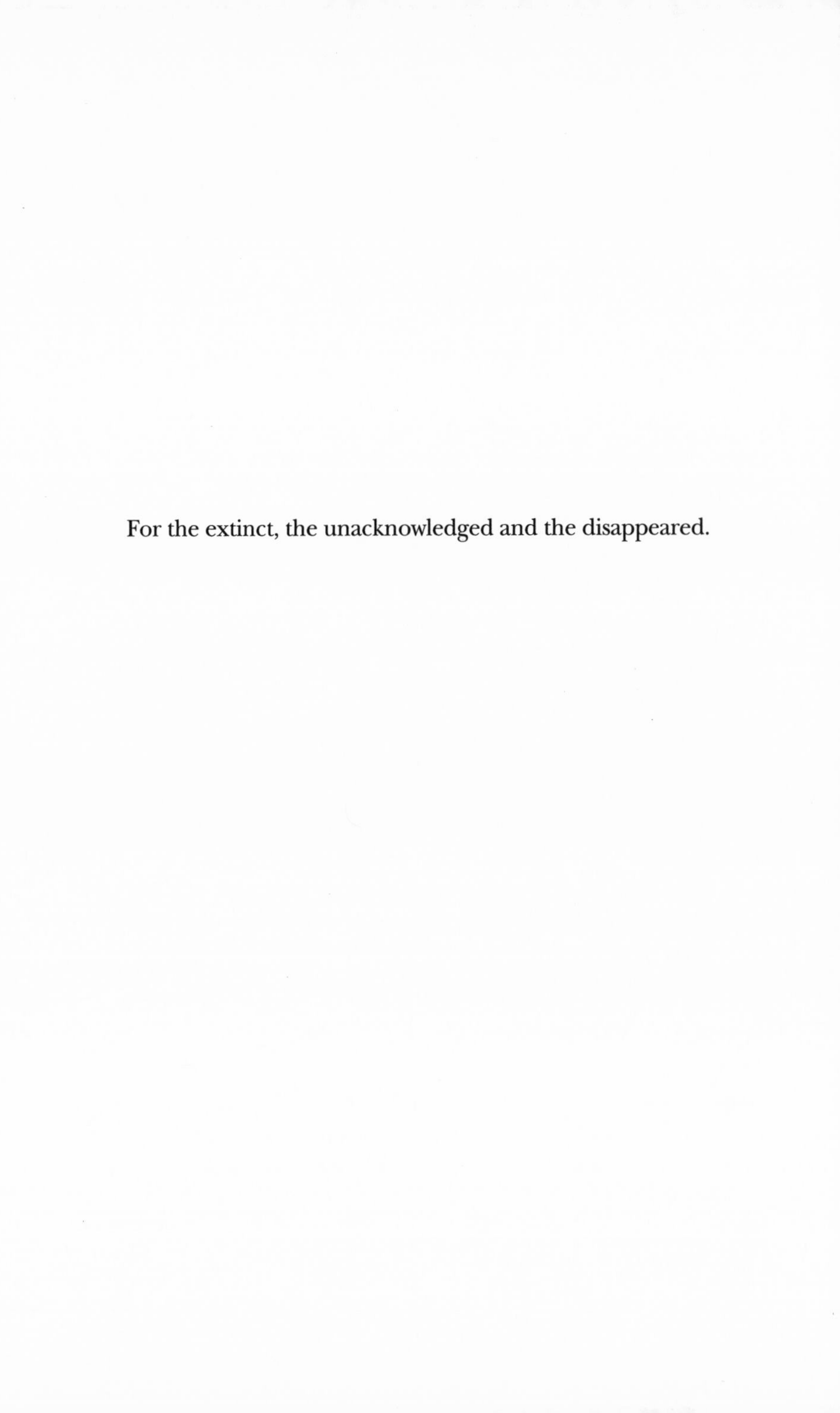

For the extinct, the unacknowledged and the disappeared.

... The relentless compass. The open sea.
The clock echoing in the memory...
The incalculable dust that was armies...
The calligrapher's meticulous line.
The suicide's face in the mirror...
The forms of a cloud in the desert.
Every arabesque in the kaleidoscope.
Each regret and each tear.
All those things were made perfectly clear
So our hands could meet.

—Jorge Luis Borges

... it cannot, I think, be doubted, that... before the paper is decayed on which this animal has been figured, it will be ranked among those species which have perished from the face of the earth.

— Charles Darwin

We who draw do so not only to make something observed visible to others, but also to accompany something invisible to its incalculable destination.

—John Berger

PROLOGUE

***Dusicyon australis:* the Falkland Islands wolf**

My kind is extinct. Time, to me, is a storm that has passed. Yet while you read, I live on in your dream.

Where am I now? In these words.

At first, after crossing the ice, I had no enemies. These islands were mine, as were their paths. I ran with my tail held high. When the first men came, their fires kept me circling. When the men in ships arrived, their fires sent me running. To them I was the fox of their homeland, the killer of lambs.

Now I paddle the cold seas of extinction, tell myself old stories to keep from drowning. A fool in life, who did not fear his destroyers, in death I run with the shamans.

I am a ravenous soul.

PART ONE

I

José Ramírez tastes blood: the remains of two teeth snapped from his jaw when Corporal Vargas punched him. A bloodied canine and a shattered lower incisor dropped into the hard-packed snow as he fell.

It's true, it was him. A boy with his hand in a barrel of food, searching for slabs of dried beef, for officers' rations, a boy who had lost a fifth of his weight and did not have more to lose. And yet he grinned when he turned around, a schoolboy proud of his defiance as his superior gripped him. Now he is dying a traitor's death.

"Goodnight, Ramírez."

José resisted. Vargas pushed him down. Eyes closed, he felt his shoulders dislocate as Vargas lashed his wrists to two stakes, then bound his feet together and lashed them to a third. An icy crucifixion. Now the officers, including Vargas, have gone, returned to the decrepit schoolhouse where they have camped for several weeks, dug in, stupidly, without adequate rations or munitions. Thirty boys from Buenos Aires Province, whose preparation consisted of a scant year's training up north. Conscripts dressed in flimsy uniforms, rewarded with rifles; a classroom of kids whose job was to starve while their superiors stuffed themselves with meat. José's empty stomach burns.

Steak and red wine. His mother's face appears in the moon, haggard and silent, the sky cobalt between clouds. He smiles. His mother smiles back, her face framed in smoke from her evening cigarette. *I saved this bottle for you. I knew you were coming.* His mother's yellow radio is on and the stars pulsate with old-fashioned dance music. José watches himself dance a few steps. His mother blushes. *You,* she says. *You are just like your father.*

His mind peels away, floats high to observe himself staked out on the snow, face up, an inert Y in helmet and boots, extremities freezing, nerves seared by shooting pains he can feel but does not attribute to the torture. This pain is different—a shimmering, a crisis.

Who am I? He is not his body. Neither is he his weapon or his uniform. From where he hovers, his mortal form is a different country. He rises up and away as his mother taps her fingers on the table. *Relax, my dear, take your time,* the salt and pepper shakers clacking together as he puts them down and lifts his fork to his mouth.

The steak she has served him is delicious. He is nineteen again, newly conscripted, his future uncertain.

His mother listens intently. He can hear her breathing down night's black telephone receiver. It slips out of his hands. He retrieves it. She is gone. Tucked back inside his helmet like a curl.

He looks down. The wind is a part of this country, as is the moon, the cold, and the ocean. The land, a folded explosion, a series of random splashes, countless little islands, their edges negotiated, revealed and obscured by the tides. Ice water welling up and mingling with warmer currents to give rise to rich algal blooms that feed legions of seabirds and mammals.

You must run, says his mother. *Run away. They will take you like they did your father.*

The steak has gone cold. They are coming for him but he cannot hide. He is a student, enrolled at the university. It is his class that will go to war. His papers come and he does what they ask. Winning this war is his chance, they say, to be a hero.

His mother will have gone to bed. His civilian friends, those who are left, will be leaving the bars. There will be a cool breeze along the avenues, the whisper of approaching winter, which freezes grapes in Mendoza and broadens the white caps of the mountains around Bariloche. In their Colegiales apartment, his father's books will still be on bookshelves, arranged according to an idiosyncratic system that is neither alphabetic nor thematic. His father's ancient *Iliad*, a faded blue hardcover with crimson endpapers, stuffed with handwritten pages of his own Spanish and Italian translations. *And so fell Patroclus, like a wild boar killed by a lion when both are angry and parched by thirst.*

Blood trickles past his ear. José imagines a chocolate bar, slightly frozen. He salivates, the candy suspended achingly over his mouth. When he gets home he will not look back. The sun sets early here on the edge of the Antarctic. The wind whips the snow against his face. He does not flinch or otherwise react.

I'm coming to get you! His father, in their apartment, 1970, taking off his spectacles and leaving them on the table. He rubs his eyes as he stands, then crouches, bending his fingers into claws. *I'm coming to get you!*

José shrieks with delight and slides under the couch. There is just enough room for him to squeeze under. Beneath, all is silent. Dust dances on the wooden boards. A marble with a red tornado inside rolls toward him. He reaches out, very slowly, takes hold of it just as his father grabs his ankles and yanks him backwards. He bangs his head on the edge of the couch before he cranes his neck and turns to look. No one is there. His father has disappeared. His shattered glasses lie on the floor. The red marble is gone.

You, says his mother, lighting another cigarette as clouds pass over the moon again and the wind rises.

❧

It has been a few hours now, and José is drifting, watching as the moon brightens; he is noticing a shadow beside him: a darkness that reveals itself to be a man.

He has thick black hair and wears an animal skin draped around his shoulders. Behind the man is a wolf with a ruddy coat and dark tail tipped with white. It seems to belong to the man, running in wide circles around him. The man takes a step, and José notices he is barefoot. He is also covered in grease, yellow fat smeared across his torso. He is young, perhaps twenty-five, and his face is scarred.

Clouds blow in. Amber and crimson explosions light up the horizon; jagged mountaintops are illuminated against the stars. José does not care. He has left his body, and from where he hovers he can see he is barely breathing. White lips that belong to Private José Ramírez, nineteen years old, beaten badly with the butt of a rifle to be made an example of. Private Ramírez, who is on the brink of death.

The animal sniffs. The stranger kneels down, pokes José and tugs at his uniform. He runs his fingers around the cords that bind José's wrists and ankles, then reaches inside his tunic and pulls out a knife, a shell blade lashed to a wooden handle. Slowly he saws at the ropes until they begin to fray.

The man's breath is warm. José looks into his brown eyes. A thick scar runs down his arm, ropy and keloid. The man saws patiently back and forth. The animal pokes its nose in José's face, licks him, then barks, and the man reaches over and clenches its muzzle. Its eyes are yellow and widely set, and two long teeth show between its jaws. It growls. The man stands up. His legs are strong, his feet calloused. He looks down at Ramírez, then squats and places his hand in front of Ramírez's mouth, checking for breath. José feels himself solidify.

He can hear his father. He is reading, slowly, in translation, a verse from his beloved *Iliad*: *Sorrow fell on Achilles like a cloud. He swept up the dust and poured it over his head. He tore his hair. And yet, despite his grief, he returned to battle, after putting on new armour.*

Time condenses into a tight band around José's nostrils. The sky is lightening, the thud of a shell exploding can be felt through the darkness. His limbs are heavy.

The man runs away over the frozen tundra. The sound of his feet hitting the snow is rhythmic and regular. The wolf is still with him, barely audible. Its paws run too lightly across the snow. They grow smaller, moving at incredible speed over the lowest slope of Mount Longdon and down toward the coast. They arrive at a beach, where the man untethers a canoe. Pushing it away from the treacherous rocks, he leaps in, the animal too, and together they disappear across the water, until there is nothing left but battleships and ocean.

A man José recognizes bends over him. It's Miguel, his friend from the training camp. He presses on José's chest, breathes into his mouth, and José inhales.

Spring, 1973. Books are piled on the coffee table, not an even tower but a haphazard monument.

"Mother will hate you for that," says José.

"What?" Carlos peers at him, incredulous. Speaking to his

father is like waking him from sleep. "José, I do not have time for this kind of nonsense."

"It isn't nonsense, Father. It's existentialism." José does not know what the word means.

"Did you change your underwear this morning?"

Carlos often asks embarrassing questions. It's his attempt to appear normal, the kind of father who attends soccer matches. Not the kind who forgets his son at the national library, as he did one Saturday morning, leaving him alone for three hours while he photocopied documents and scrolled through microfiches, only to run into him again by accident in the middle of a stairwell.

The library was huge. Or that's how it seemed to a boy left to his own devices. Its geometric shape defied logic. Serious young people strolled along its corridors cradling books in their arms. José walked taller as he strode among them, imagining the books he might carry—probably cartoon annuals, his preferred reading. Or empty sketchbooks, filled with the possibility of what might be drawn. José had discovered the biology section, where huge books of photographs of animals were pressed together, arctic against equatorial, predator against prey. He took his tracing paper and pencils and sat on the rough carpet tiles with his tongue protruding, meticulously tracing sharks and boa constrictors, axolotls, antelopes and macaques. It was perfect: no interruptions, no chores or meals; just the faint flickering of the lights. Quiet.

José's silence makes his father forget about him. Sometimes José wishes he were the kind of boy who knocked books off shelves, ran up and down the aisles and climbed on the furniture, struck up conversations with mumbling vagrants, and found a way to break into the vending machines and steal the chewing gum. He knows boys like that. But he's not one of them.

He is not sure what he is, which genus or species.

He draws to define himself. He also daydreams. Imagines himself in the jungle or the Arctic, discovering creatures no one has dreamed about and then being interviewed on evening television. *Look,* his mother will one day shout, the pasta unwinding from her fork. *Carlos, darling, it's José!* And his father will look up. *My word,* he'll remark, *look at our talented son.*

Sometimes, at the end of the day, José crawls into his father's lap and shows him his drawings. Sometimes his father listens and laughs. But other times he just stares into space, and José has to pinch him to get his attention. Sometimes José feels a ball of hatred forming inside his stomach.

José's sketches accumulate, tucked beneath the mattress of his bed. That is his wild life. He also has a civilized one. At school, he does well. He is the smartest boy, and he's not stuck-up. His schoolmates like him. They tease him about his skinny legs, but they also admire his drawings and his impersonations of other kids and the teachers. José can be funny. He can turn on the charm, pull a funny face, or think of the right thing to say at an awkward moment. This saves him from bullies. Nevertheless, he lives on a knife edge.

"Hey, Ramírez, does your father ever smile?"

"Hey, Ramírez, does your dad know your mother's a hippie?"

"Of course he does! They belong to the same swingers club."

They laugh, but he doesn't trust them. They don't trust him. No one trusts anyone. It's the seventies. His father is an intellectual, his mother a former trade unionist. At school there's an atmosphere of hysteria, suppressed by jokes and the formation of intense cliques. As he grows older, José begins to keep his drawings in three different places: a folder he displays on the tiny desk in his bedroom, another folder under his mattress, and a third hidden behind a panel in his closet. He does not need to hide them. His pictures are dreamy and fantastical, or meticulously real, never controversial.

Secrets are all around, and he wants his own.

His parents never speak about work. They do not show affection. He knows that much is missing from the way they touch. Their hearts are locked in the stacks, hearts that must be handled with white cotton gloves.

Pencils. How he loves them, lives for their range of intensities. A day of joy or frustration is 4B or 6B; a day of dreams and meandering, 2H, 4H. The middle ground of HB is reserved for school, where conventionality is paramount. The HB pencil is for capturing the acceptable mid-range of emotion, for writing legible and reasonable words, not easily erased, words not carved too deep or smudged too wide. But at night, in his room, or at the kitchen table while his mother washes up and his father sits in his office, José brings out the wooden box that contains multitudes—colours and shades, erasers and sharpeners—and fills his sketchbook with jungles, deserts and plains.

"I hope you do not think you are going to art school."

His mother makes remarks like this when she sees him sharpening pencils or leafing through pages of sketches. She wants to make it quite clear that art is dangerous. And stupid. A complete waste of time. This is, in part, a dig at his father. She is worried. She does not want her son to end up with his head in the clouds like his father. She worked for most of her twenties in a sewing machine factory and is proud of it. She knows where she comes from and wants José to know it: they are peasants. Once they used to farm, but now they are city dwellers. She has worked with her hands, screwing tiny metal pieces together, worked with her mind, overseeing others, drafting union documents. In her youth, she read and wrote poetry. That was when she met Carlos. Together they published pamphlets until Carlos got hired at the university and dedicated himself to translating and teaching. They both agree that drawing isn't work. It wouldn't bring in money, or at least not enough to rely on.

"Of course not," José says. "I am going to be a scientist."

"Not a worker?"

"Scientists work."

"That is just a bourgeois fantasy."

"What about the people who make their test tubes? The women who launder and starch their beloved lab coats?"

"Science is a collective endeavour, José, and for that reason should be nationalized, so that we can all play our part in it."

"What about Papa? He works alone."

Rosa puts her hands on her hips and José's chest swells with excitement. Once again, he has won. She cannot argue with that.

José sharpens a pencil. The grace of a fine curl of wood. How long can he extend it before it breaks? The delicate, scalloped edge of paint, the scent of lead and cedar that emerges from it. If he's not careful he will go too far and leave the lead exposed. It's a tricky business.

José does not listen to her words. They are remnants of the socialist rain that fell on his country. At least she speaks. His father barely opens his mouth at all. As José grows up and becomes more independent, he is left alone in their modest apartment every Saturday. By the age of ten, he's a regular in the neighbourhood bookstores, purchasing or pilfering what he can of his beloved art books, as well as the occasional prized *National Geographic*. He has also discovered other libraries and has learned to pick up discarded magazines from people's garbage. He and his father grow apart. No longer small enough to fit on his lap, José leaves drawings lying on books or interleaves them between his father's documents. More often than not, he finds them crumpled up, tossed into a corner several days later.

"Your father does not mean to hurt your feelings," Rosa whispers after José thumps the table in frustration. "He is very busy. He is preoccupied."

It's strange how his mother defends his father, even when she and José accuse him of the same things: abandoning his family in favour of his research, being ill-mannered, inconsiderate, morose. They argue loudly. Sometimes his mother slaps his father in an attempt to get him to react. José watches but never intervenes. Instead he hovers, pressed against walls, his hands deep in his pockets, fidgeting nervously. *I must pay attention,* he tells himself. *This is important.* He is observing the behaviour of two endangered mammals.

October 7, 1977. Rosa comes home early from her new job at the hospital. Carlos is putting the finishing touches on yet another paper he is writing on Spanish translations of James Joyce, to be delivered at a conference in Barcelona. He does not go to his university office because he isn't feeling well. He's due to fly out in three days and is battling a headache and fever.

Or so he says. Rosa cannot feel any difference between his forehead and hers. She also suspects he has been drinking lately. She smells liquor on his breath when he gets home late. She wonders if he might be having an affair. José knows all this because she tells him afterwards, sitting beside him on the couch and handing him a glass of maté.

"You have to know this, you are almost a man." He doesn't feel like one, his giant feet stick out awkwardly in front of him like a puppet's on the ends of sticks.

His mother runs up the three flights of stairs to their apartment and finds the door open. She goes inside and sees papers lying everywhere, as if a wind has blown through. A sandwich sits uneaten on the low table.

She calls out to her husband. No response.

Later that evening, sometime after nine, a neighbour knocks on the door. She is holding Carlos's glasses, which she has found lying in the alley.

"I think these might be your husband's," says the older woman. She has only recently moved into the apartment below, and they have not formally introduced themselves. "My name is Ana," she says.

José's mother examines the fine cracks in the lenses. Otherwise the spectacles appear unharmed. "Did you see him?" she asks.

"No."

José's mother is convinced Ana was involved. "There was a gleam in her eye," she says.

All José knows of Ana is that she often sits in the hallway watching people come and go, her hands knotting and unknotting in her lap.

José's mother visits the police station every day the following week, demanding to know what happened. The cops laugh.

"Look in the mirror," they say. "Clearly, Rosa Ramírez, your husband has left you for a younger woman." They spit in her face and tell her to go home. She visits the university next and refuses to leave until both the dean of the faculty and the chancellor agree to see her.

"Don't you understand?" they say. "We cannot talk to you about this."

Leaving, she catches the eye of the dean. His pupils open up into chasms before he blinks and she looks away.

She stays up at night, talking on the phone or writing letters. She examines every one of Carlos's papers, page after page of typewritten lecture notes, translations and essay drafts. It's impossible, she tells José. Why would they take him? His father is no longer a radical, he has become too cautious. Sentences of convoluted Spanish peppered with question marks drift to the hardwood floor. She is the one who talks about politics. She is the one who follows what passes as news. Every day when she buses to her new job at the hospital she picks up the latest gossip from her companions. Gossip that is trivial but filled with clues. Surely it's she they meant to kidnap.

That summer, José becomes serious. He stops spending time with his friends. He gets a part-time job working in an art supply store where he sells coloured markers. He stops drawing imaginary animals and instead allows himself to draw only what he can see. He draws trucks and billboards, beggars and trees, benches and passing pedestrians, all with care. He aims for technical precision rather than emotional exactness—the perfect translation of visual experience. He does not cry. Some days the sensation of his arm moving is the only thing that tells him he is alive.

11

In 1979, José shows his drawings to a girl at school named Gaby. Gaby is shy and wears cat-eye glasses. She sits behind him in math and biology, and her gaze resting on his back causes him to itch such that he cannot concentrate. He conjures up her image—a tall girl with long braids whose breasts push against her blouse, causing the gaps between buttons to bulge slightly. He turns around and looks at her and then glances away. Her face is pretty.

Gaby lives not too far from his apartment complex, over near the train tracks. One warm afternoon he runs into her outside the El Sol Café and impulsively invites her to sit down with him. They order two black coffees that neither drink. Gaby plays with the sugar packets while José reaches inside his pocket and pulls out some drawings of local storefronts: a bakery, a flea market.

"These are amazing," says Gaby. Her eyes are wide. A breeze flutters the tablecloth, and a waft of jacaranda mixed with the buttery smell of fresh medialunas fills José's nostrils.

"Thank you," he says, keen to be polite.

"Do you draw portraits?" asks Gaby. "You could charge money for them."

"Not often." He gathers up the drawings, shoves them back into his pockets.

"Would you like to take a walk?"

They walk down side streets toward Avenida Santa Fe. Gaby impersonates their biology teacher who has a way of emphasizing all the wrong syllables. Near the park, they grow silent. José puts his arm around Gaby's shoulders and kisses her.

Gaby shrieks. A lizard has run up her leg. She shakes it off and the two of them laugh, kissing again. They continue to kiss as if it is their new way of breathing. When Gaby kisses José, he feels intoxicated. She leans toward him, pressing her breasts against his chest. Her clothes are neat, close-fitting.

They meet outdoors, near the Palermo woods, or elsewhere near the university where they can sometimes find a place to sit under the trees. Once in a while Gaby wears jeans and José slips his fingers under the waistband, touches the elastic edge of her underwear, only to feel her pull away. It's a game of hide-and-seek. He never invites her home, although he longs to. He imagines her kneeling beside his father's books, taking them out to read. It's a dangerous thought. Gaby does not seem interested in showing him her home either, although he knows where she lives and often walks her to the steps of her apartment building, hoping she will change her mind. He likes the idea of meeting her parents and older brothers. He would show them how serious he is. He would not put his arm around Gaby but stay close to her, and the brothers would catch each other's eyes and exchange nods. He would pass the test.

When they reach her building, Gaby turns and offers a final kiss, not the deep kind that massages his whole tongue but a chaste peck, like a sister's, on his forehead. Then she flounces up the steps and opens the door, letting it swing closed behind her. After a few minutes, she appears at a third- floor window.

He recognizes her hair: the long braid swung over her left shoulder. She never looks down. She raises or lowers the window, gazes across the street, or turns her back and leaves him to imagine who she is talking to. José's lips swell, exhausted from all that kissing. He has to rub them with the back of his hand, agonized and frustrated. Then he walks for hours.

Rosa might ask where he's been, but she does not seem to worry. She's too preoccupied, smoking and drinking in the kitchen while she talks on the telephone, or working her way through mountains of paperwork, badly photocopied, smudged.

Perhaps she thinks José is of no interest to the government. But the government does not care about interesting. The government does not discriminate. Already two young women who lived in their building have disappeared, and no one has suggested a reason. No one reacted at all.

When Gaby finally invites him home, it's not what he expects. Her parents are out and her brothers, it turns out, do not live at home. One is a ranch hand and the other is in Buenos Aires, working for a theatre company. Her apartment is small and full of little objects: brass candlesticks, ceramic figurines and the like. A nightmare to dust, his mother would say, the kind of place where a grandmother lives, surrounded by reminders of the past.

Her hallway smells of cooking and cigarette smoke, a trace of cologne.

"I have made arrangements," she says and smiles. He notices she's wearing lipstick. He will have to wash his face before he leaves.

"I am ready," she says enigmatically and leads him into her bedroom, a tiny room with a cot and a chest of drawers, a picture of the crucifixion.

He does not know what she means and he feels a little stupid. Not knowing where to put himself, he sits down on the bed. It's very firm. He wonders how she can sleep on it. In contrast to the rest of the house, her room is severe, not at all the place he imagined, full of perfume and confusing undergarments. Out the window he sees the familiar street: peeling colonial house fronts with cast-iron balconies, a lonely yellow dog scavenging for scraps.

Gaby starts undressing. She begins at the top, pulling the pins out of her hair, and works her way down, unbuttoning her blouse and laying it beside her on a chair, expertly slipping off her bra which appears to be heavily upholstered, for when it falls away her breasts are small, their brown globes suspended against her chest.

José reaches over and touches them. First one, then the other, shyly and slowly, stroking them until Gaby slaps him away.

It seems he has to wait until she is naked. He turns away and looks at Christ, impassive and self-involved up on his crucifix. Is that what it means to suffer? To be nailed in place and to think the same sad thoughts over and over?

When he turns around she is lying on the bed, her hair spread out around her on the pillow. José cannot believe how much of it there is. He averts his eyes and takes off his clothes, and for a moment stands transfixed, Gaby's gaze suspending him before she lifts the sheet and José slides in beside her, thinking for some reason that Christ must have had multiple erections, given that he was human.

He cannot breathe. She turns toward him, her eyes lowered. Her breasts brush his chest and abdomen; he takes the nipples, one after the other, into his mouth. Slowly, very slowly, she presses the length of her body into his. He runs his hand down her belly, feels the little hairs along her midline grow thicker as his hand moves further down. He strokes her labia, and then, with great solemnity, she pulls him into her. He is overtaken by his own desire. Gaby lifts her chin, closes her eyes.

Afterwards, Gaby gets up, her strong back and slender buttocks disappearing swiftly behind a towel as she makes her way to the bathroom. While José waits for her to return, the smell of coffee fills the apartment. He has just started buttoning his shirt when he hears the apartment door open. He can hear Gaby's father, solemn, as if returning home from a funeral.

"Good afternoon," he says.

José had been hoping to pull Gaby back to bed. Instead he must join her for coffee, during which her father quizzes her ferociously about her schoolwork and periodically glares at José.

"What did you do today, my son?" Rosa asks.

"Nothing," says José, turning away. He wants badly to confide in her. She might think he had pushed Gaby into it. Or that she would laugh.

His hands shake. "I have met a girl."

Rosa smiles, then catches herself. "Be careful. Who is her father? Does he work for the military?"

"No," says José. "He runs a tailoring business."

"I see." Rosa takes off her apron and leans against the table. "Are they Catholic?"

"Yes."

Rosa smiles.

José smiles back. "Perhaps she could come over for dinner?" His voice rises.

"No, José, not now."

"What do you mean?" José stands.

"You know what I mean." Now they are facing each other.

Rosa's voice is harsh, but her eyes have flooded. "If you're thinking of Papi, forget it. He's not coming back."

"How do you know? People reappear."

"Just like Jesus." Rosa covers her mouth and turns away and begins to cry.

José's jaw clenches. Why does she have to spoil this for him? Can they not be normal just for a while? It's as if his skin has been cracked, and now he is exposed, a vulnerable sac of organs. If this is what making love does to you, he does not understand why people do it. Nevertheless, he wants to do it again.

"Does she have blue eyes?"

"What? No, they are dark. Why do you care, anyway?"

"I am your mother," she smiles. "I am supposed to ask questions." Her body softens. A curl springs out from behind her ear.

His mother does not want to meet Gaby, but wants to hear about her. José shows her some of his drawings. He thinks she will be horrified—some are semi-nudes—but it seems she is comforted from seeing the care he has taken with them.

He tells Gaby about his mother's interest, embarrassed by the peculiarity of it, yet also glad to broach the subject. Gaby says she does not mind. At least his mother is not angry with him. Her own father, she says, does not want her to have any boyfriends. If not a doctor, he wants her to be a lawyer, an idea which repulses Gaby. Her mother is more relaxed, saying Gaby can do what she likes so long as she studies.

"Lawyers are all crooks," she says. "Doesn't he know that?"

"Some aren't," says José. His mother is friends with a lawyer who works for the unions.

Gaby speaks in hushed tones about her cousin Ramón who was a student at the university before he disappeared on his way home from a lecture about Freud. José draws her during their conversations. He draws her when they are apart. He draws her obsessively, hour after hour, wearing down pencils while burning through paper he steals from the school art cupboard. No one seems to notice. Art is not popular. The teacher is always hungover. He drones endlessly on about hot and cold colours, the importance of producing an accurate colour wheel. As a result, no one uses much paper.

Meanwhile the garbage can in José's bedroom overflows with shavings, their fragrant woodiness. José sometimes masturbates over his sketches. He's careful not to get semen on them. He draws Gaby every week. They meet at her apartment when her parents are gone, which is fairly often as they both work long hours. José begins to use the sketches as a kind of diary, capturing with the quality of his lines the kind of sex they are having—views of Gaby from the back, side and front, up against a wall or draped over a chair—and his drawing skills improve tremendously. It's as if the distraction of his arousal helps him to see more clearly, the charcoal breaking into cinders as the oils of his fingers merge with soot and ash and push the darkness into the paper.

Sometimes Gaby appears taut, her muscles and bones angular, and her eyes focused. Other times her flesh is soft, blurred, and she looks away, her head to one side, as if unwilling to face what the day demands, angled light slipping through the slats in a blind. Sometimes he puts away his pastels and pencils and takes his old rusty nib and ink along to draw her fully clothed. These are the sketches he shows his mother—innocent yet erotically evocative.

"Your father would write me letters," Rosa says, "after we met."

"Where was that?"

"In class. When I didn't go back, he delivered them by hand. A letter every day for two whole months."

"What did your mother think?" José rubs at the ink stains on his fingers.

"I never told her."

"Do you still have them—the letters?"

"No," said his mother. "I destroyed them."

José thinks he will never destroy his drawings. He already knows they are significant to him in a way that even Gaby might not always be.

José sketches strangers. The act of looking means he does not need to think, only inhabit what he sees. Men in raincoats, old women seated on park benches, children fighting unheeded in the dusty gutter. He also inhabits plants—weeds picked from between paving stones—crushed pop cans and empty cigarette cartons.

The portraits arrive on the paper.

Gaby grows critical. "This one is beautiful," she says, "but this one needs to be darker. Her arms are too light." She refers to the woman in the drawings in the third person, as if it has nothing to do with her. José respects this. He labels his sketches impersonally: "Woman Undressing," or "Woman with Raised Arms." It's an empty exercise, for how can he forget? With every mark, her contours shape his art.

One Saturday morning, after they have been seeing each other for several weeks, they take the train out to Tigre, the ramshackle river town north of the city, where Gaby's uncle Tomás has a waterfront house. "Tomás is an artist, like you." Gaby folds his fingers into hers on the juddering train.

Tomás, it turns out, is a drunk who only gets up at night when the river is full of assassins' shadows. José and Gaby sleep together in a hammock slung between two bulbous silk floss trees. By day, José wanders Tomás's darkened rooms, which are plastered with garish paintings of jaguars and snakes.

"No one in the family speaks to him now," admits Gaby,

smoking in her bathing suit on the dangerously rotten veranda. "But he was always my favourite. He brought me candies."

They swim in the river, and later cook the sausages they brought. Tomás grins, his grizzled face speckled with grease. He hasn't eaten this well, he concedes, since he left the city two years ago. But when José beckons him inside, to the room filled with paintings, the older artist shakes his head and turns away.

"I hope you don't end up like him," says Gaby, as they wait at the station. They have both lied to their families about where they were going. On the train back, they find an empty compartment and make love twice, between stations, and by the end, Gaby is laughing uncontrollably. She's still grinning as she disappears into her house.

Six months before he leaves for the Malvinas, he comes upon a small charcoal sketch pressed in the pages of an old atlas, between the halves of a map of the world's populations in shades of red and yellow. It's been eighteen months since they broke up. The woman is seated, looking down, her hair loose in front of her face with only her nose and chin visible. Her fingers are slender and articulate, one hand resting upon the other. Looking at the image, José feels a shiver of pride followed by an intense wave of nostalgia. He is nineteen now, no longer the sixteen-year-old she fell in love with. Gaby—the woman in the sketch, the girl, for she is terribly young, her life not yet touched by cynicism.

"We are grown now," she said the evening they parted. It was winter, and Gaby was carrying a bag of groceries: day-old bread and a jar of pickled herring. "The memories are very beautiful, but we've run out of time."

He has not signed the picture. This is true of many of his portraits, which will make it easier, when the time comes, to dispose of them quickly, to rip them into pieces and throw them in the incinerator along with his mother's classified union documents. He is going to be a soldier. He cannot love.

Perhaps this is how it will be when I am fifty, he thinks, burning love letters and destroying evidence. Isn't that the fate of many men? For a moment, he wonders if his father was just an adulterer, an ordinary coward who cracked under the strain of maintaining two lives. José fills the emptiness his father left with images, some of them heroic, others demonic.

José sees Gaby the week before he leaves town for training camp. She has cut her hair. It doesn't suit her, but he compliments it anyway. He notices her clothes are also new. He asks about her job and she says she likes it, although he doubts this. She's too intelligent to enjoy being a typist.

"You should have these," he says. He hands over the remaining sketches he did of her, mostly from the back, sitting in a chair. In one or two she is naked, but the drawings are modest. If he does not come back, he hopes the drawings will comfort her. Gaby has a new boyfriend from the office where she works. He is twenty-seven. Perhaps she is better off with a civilian. But José is sure Gaby still dreams of him, because sometimes when he wakes at night he hears her breathing, even here, a thousand miles away.

III

José's eyes open into twilight, a sharp pain in his lungs. He feels himself lifted up, slung over someone's shoulder, head hanging down, swinging back and forth, the motion making him retch. Then the foxhole: thick with men's flatus and bad breath. Dark still, freezing, and full of clicking weapons. Miguel lays José down on a wet bedroll. Miguel lifts a canteen to José's lips and José swallows several mouthfuls of icy water.

There is no Rosa now, no moon and no wolf, only the familiar dark. José feels his pulse against his skin, cannot feel his feet and fingers. The pain begins to rise.

Remember, whispers the wolf.

Unsure of where he is, he lifts his head.

They have left him alone in the dark.

Later, Miguel brings him soup but he can't stomach it. Miguel settles on the ground beside José and they lie together, shoulder to shoulder. "You need to get warm. You must get warm now."

José feels Miguel's heat. Then his weight, as he slides on top of him. The pressure of another body is comforting, agonizing. José closes his eyes. He feels the man's hands moving up and down his body, Miguel's movements becoming more and more erratic. He begins to rub himself against José's legs, then stops. José feels the man's rib cage shudder with tight, hard sobs. José's body is aroused, his mind confused.

The men listen to the distant sounds of gunfire.

"They will take the mountain," whispers Miguel, a man with an aquiline nose, the profile of Nero. José closes his eyes, imagines a plumed helmet, a beaten gold breastplate, a long spear. He wears the crucifix his mother gave him but has not prayed since Carlos disappeared.

Miguel massages José's arms. José wishes only to be dead. It is too hard to be touched with such need, especially in the midst of so much filth: rotten feet, abandoned corpses, frozen latrines. José feels shame. Wishes he could laugh. Back in training camp, he learned that Miguel sold shoes in his civilian life. That he worked for his father in Barracas, slipping cheap sandals on and off the swollen feet of factory workers, complimenting the style of old men who insist on heels. He learned about Miguel's many girlfriends, saw the photos of their beautiful faces and blond hair. Miguel is twenty-one, one of the older conscripts. José imagines bringing Miguel home and introducing him to his mother. No doubt she would make a fuss of him, especially if he brought her a pair of shoes. She likes to wear heels once in a while. She used to joke that she needed to look her husband in the eye. When they came home from an evening out, José would hear her laughing. This was before his father grew morose, in the early days when he would leave his work at the office and came home human. *And after the battle Achilles laid himself to rest with the beautiful Briseis beside him.*

The others are descending into the foxhole. Cold air penetrates. "I can't move my hands," says José. "I can't feel my feet."

Miguel unlaces José's boots and attempts to slip them off, but then seems to think better of it. For a short while they don't speak, then an explosion rips past, somewhere down below, and suddenly Vargas's voice can be heard, calling them to battle.

José can't imagine fighting. "Go and join the others," he says to Miguel. "I will be okay. I will try to follow."

Their country is at war with itself. Gaby turned serious when José told her he had been conscripted. She cried. He remembers the urgent pressure of her lips. What would she think if she knew where he was, what he'd done?

Quickly, Miguel leaves, and in his wake, in the small circle of sky outside the foxhole, a brief constellation of sparks flashes.

I have disappeared, thinks José. *I have become the number sewn on the sleeve of my shirt.* In the stink and sink of the peat, there is no one to hold him. The night has returned and snow is blowing, mixed with rain. Painfully, he sits up, rolls over and pushes himself up onto his knees. And then like a dog, he crawls out into the cold.

Miguel said they were taking the mountain, the mountain they've held for weeks. A grenade flies overhead, explodes twenty feet away. The force of the explosion throws José to the ground.

His ears ring. *This is it,* whispers his father, somewhere, *now you are on your own.* José shudders, imagines Carlos's eyes staring out from behind their lenses.

He gets back onto his hands and knees. He can no longer tell if it is day or night. The ridge is a mass of smoke cut through by small arms fire. The camp, protected by deserted farm buildings, forms the only bridge between him and the battlefield. José crawls on, hoping to reach it. He must be invisible. The enemy are attacking and his comrades are at their command posts. He can almost recognize Mendes and Cabral. Their backs are to him. No one else came for him because they thought he was dead or would die soon. Brits are running in all directions, dodging small arms fire as they gain the ridge.

José continues to crawl his way between explosions to a crumbling wall. He calls out to Mendes and Cabral but they cannot hear him. They look right through him. It's as if he is a ghost. Then Cabral is hit. His body flails, rolls away, flips down the hillside. José tries to stand, but his feet do not work. They are frozen. He is nothing. No weapon, no position, and nowhere to run. He should have died where he was staked. He must find a place to wait it out.

A flare illuminates Vargas, stretching Carlos's arms apart across a metal frame.

Don't worry, Josito, whispers Carlos toward his son, his ribs visible through his shirt, and straining. *Go back to your soldiering. This is all just a dream.*

A man screams wildly. His cry is cut off. A Brit has stuck his bayonet deep into his abdomen, twisting it around until his insides spill and nothing can be done. *And so fell Patroclus.*

José presses himself flat to the ground, grinds his face into the freezing mud. It's too far for him to reach the farm, its stone walls and fragments of roof unable to protect him anyway. I am dead, he thinks.

A Brit yells. José holds his breath. Men stampede past him like cattle, heading for the abandoned camp. He sees their boots, sturdier than his, their powerful feet and legs. They say these men will eat you if they capture you. They will roast you on a spit and drink your blood. They are wild dogs, simple as that, without conscience or morality. Their pink heads are full of murder and they will stop at nothing to get their way. They stink like rotten meat and drink warm beer. The British are insane, cowardly, and serve a screaming martinet in a blond wig, a woman so ugly and cruel she makes Perón's wives seem angelic. At least Argentina's women are beautiful. At least they know their place, and how to dress. José's grandmother was a Peronist. She refused to hear anything bad about the man despite his betrayal of his people.

José hears a thud. Has something pierced him? He opens his eyes. A Brit stands over him with a bayonet, its end bloody. José puts his head down. He prays to his father that the man doesn't see him and glances up again: the whites of the man's eyes are lit by orange flares.

Something else catches the light—an animal, trotting heedlessly between explosions, its mouth open, tongue hanging out, a wedge-headed dog finding its way between the dead. José watches the animal approach. The next time the earth lights up, the Brit is kneeling, face pressed into its dank fur. José closes his eyes.

A hand reaches out, takes hold of his upper arm and rolls him over. He hears a voice speaking, shouting. The words are garbled English. Tentatively, José touches his side, the place where the bayonet entered—but there is barely any wetness, just a long rip in his fatigues. It stings. He opens his eyes. Another Brit, red-faced and fair, is kneeling beside him, offering up a battered water canteen. José drinks. Most of it spills, soaking his jacket. The Brit's teeth flash, dog fur brushes against José's cheek and then a loud explosion flattens everything. In that slow collapse, José glimpses his father rising from the metal grill and shaking hands with Vargas.

My son is making love with the enemy, he laughs. *Our work is over.*

When José wakes again, it is completely dark. The battle has journeyed several miles westward. He can hear it, can see the limp flare of explosives reflecting off the ridges of ice that surround him, the mud freezing as the temperature drops.

A man moans. José lifts his head. An Argentine lies only a few feet away, his face a mass of blood and shattered bone. If only I could shoot, José thinks. I would put the poor bastard out of his misery. But his hands don't work and his gun is still in the foxhole, as is his ammunition and his grenade. His right side is sticky. Perhaps a few ribs are broken. He feels surprisingly alive. I will get out of here. I will return to the apartment and rescue Achilles. I will memorize his struggle and recite it every day until my father returns. No man will hurl him to this death!

Helmets, boots, and bodies lie. A rustle, followed by a click. Over there—a soldier, not the Brit who offered up his canteen, but another—walking through the chaos, dragging his left foot, wild-eyed. He crouches down a few feet away, holds up a small camera.

He is taking photographs of corpses.

José reaches for his missing gun. He does his best to take aim but the shot is wide and the gun is only his broken finger. The British soldier lifts his weapon, a bullet flies, another hits the wall. José puts up his hands.

The soldier is tall and heavy-set, probably a hundred pounds heavier than José. His face is smeared with dirt. José closes his eyes and pretends to faint. He hears the man walk up to him, frozen mud cracking under his boots. *Don't shoot,* José thinks.

The soldier kneels down and begins to unlace José's boots. José bites his tongue to avoid crying out. The pain of having his feet touched is unbearable. First the left boot and then the right are unlaced and eased off, almost tenderly, exposing José's feet to the freezing air. *He must think I'm dead.* José tries not to breathe.

It is said the Brits will treat you well, will take care of you if they take you prisoner, will feed you and tend your wounds, will not torture you, or stake you out in the snow, hoping you'll die. José does not believe this. They are thieves. They are the pigs who dare lay claim to this territory that is as far away from Britain as the Orkney Islands are from Argentina. What they want makes no sense.

The Brit is retreating, José's boots strung around his neck. José crawls across the ice, frozen corpses littering the way to the deserted farm buildings. There will be shelter from the wind. Others had the same idea. Two or three men, each slightly wounded, are huddled together there. One has managed to light a small fire and they argue about whether this is a good idea or not.

"We may as well send up a flare."

"Let them come," says one, whose arm hangs down bloody and useless. "It's time to surrender."

José shudders uncontrollably.

"Are you a coward?" asks another voice. Miguel. It is Miguel, who rises to his feet, stumbles, falls. He is wounded. José beckons him. Briefly, they embrace.

"My friend," says Miguel, "you are clearly immortal. What has happened to your boots?"

"A Brit took them."

Miguel's forehead is split open and his left eye swollen.

José whispers, "Have you seen a wolf?" Miguel does not hear. He holds a filthy rag up to his head, grimaces, and José notices bloody pulp where his front teeth used to be.

One day, Carlos would say, *we will be treated as heroes.*

Hours after the fire burns out, they are discovered. It seems the battle has been lost. After gathering the others, a British officer gestures to José to stand up, and prods him with the butt of his rifle. José's stockinged feet catch on the ice. Miguel comes to José's aid, and together they walk forward over the ridge.

It's a long march. José drifts. Is the war over? His hands are balls of thorns. His feet are on fire.

Eventually they reach the collecting point near Stanley. It is busy, organized. A padre José does not recognize says a quick mass before urging them, pointlessly, to return and fight. Then a Brit pushes them one by one into a large tent where another group Argentinian POWs are huddled. They are afraid and look pathetic: thin, filthy, and smooth-cheeked, their ill-fitting uniforms hanging off them. Teenagers, mostly. José takes his place on the floor and lowers his head. I am not dead, he thinks.

They sit in silence. Some appear to be praying. They are given food: tins of cold meat and beans, hot soup, hot chocolate. José feels his stomach convulse, his hands drop the spoon, unable to close on it, his fingers hugely swollen and blistered.

"What is wrong with your hands?"

"Frozen."

"Why?"

José tries to laugh but can't.

Another POW feeds José a spoonful of beans. Tears burn his eyes. His stomach turns. Where is Miguel? They have been separated. He misses his friend. He turns away, faces outside where the snow is coming down again. It is a torment to watch the others eat.

"Drink," says the other POW, who shoves a mug of something under his chin, tips it up so the steam burns José's eyes and the hot liquid—chocolate—runs down into his throat. It sears, but he doesn't care, he is so thirsty, and it warms him. He is so cold—he will never warm up, never return.

His tongue runs around the rim of the cup, tasting the

sweet tin. José vomits—stringy, pinkish spew.

The night that follows is the coldest he remembers.

In the morning, a British medic visits their camp. When it's his turn, the doctor gestures, and an Argentine who understands some English is brought forward. One day I will master this language, thinks José. He pictures his father's Greek and Latin dictionaries on their shelves. How he once pretended to be a police officer and dusted the backs of the dining room chairs and the knob of the door handle with flour. His mother screamed and beat him for messing up her furniture. Later it became a story they told of him, of their serious son, keen to get to the bottom of things. A story his mother stopped telling after his father disappeared.

"You have frostbite," the POW translates. "This finger is practically dead."

"Yes," says José, avoiding looking at his hands.

"The doctor wishes to see your feet."

José lifts his feet. Slowly the doctor pulls off each sock. Black, blood-filled blisters cover his toes.

The doctor says something. "You must wait here," the soldier explains. He and the doctor disappear and José is left alone with his feet, wondering if what will follow will involve more pain. When he opens his eyes, men in British uniforms are lying beside him. One is unconscious. The other's burned face is painted white. José shuts his eyes. He must be in the kelper field hospital. The British have taken him. Miguel said they liked to eat Argentinian flesh. At the time, José had laughed, but it was only bravado, his insides shrinking. Now he does not care. Let them eat, so long as he cannot feel. He has had enough of waiting for the worst. He imagines Christ, dressed in a camouflage loincloth, pushing an intravenous pole between the cots. *Jesus, forgive us.*

He is not eaten. Instead he is treated for severe frostbite, dehydration and shock, and transferred to the SS *Uganda* along with other wounded POWs. There is a doctor who speaks a little Spanish, and another Argentine appears who is not only fluent in English, but who speaks it with what sounds like a native accent. He tells José that his father is from England, but moved to Argentina to live with his mother, whose grandparents were also British. His name is Javier. Like José, he escaped from his platoon and went in search of food only to be found and taken prisoner. The Brits were confused when they heard him speak English. He described their cities in detail. Now they are using him to translate for the other POWs.

José nods. He is too exhausted to speak. He has not been asked to explain the rope burns around his wrists or ankles, or the extent of his frostbite, and does not wish to.

"Have you ever seen a wolf?" he asks Javier. "A wolf on the islands?"

"No," laughs Javier. "There are none."

José asks Javier to help him sit up. He is feeling good today after a dose of morphine.

"How long have I been here?" he asks.

"Two days."

José looks around. This is not bad, he thinks. I am warm and alive. His hands and feet are bandaged and splinted. His side aches. A trail of stars follows whenever he moves his head. But there is nothing he needs to do. He sits and watches. Another soldier in another bed, bigger and older than José, British. The British and the Argentines are mingled together in this place. No one seems to care.

The man looks familiar: something about the shape of his jaw, his forehead. Eventually it comes to him: he is the man who took his boots and also his photograph, the man who declared him dead.

The boots at rest beside the man's bed are British. What did he do with José's? Rage rises up. To hell with that moment of kindness: all Brits are thieves and the roll of film with his image on it must be somewhere, unless it has been burned, or else fallen into some puddle. José is consumed with an urge to find it. But he can't walk. His bandaged feet and legs will not cooperate.

"What are you doing?"

A nurse directs him back to bed, reattaches his intravenous line and handcuffs him to the side of his cot. She administers a shot, and when José wakes up the Brit has gone.

The next day British soldiers prance about, slap and hug each other. There is something disgusting about them—their heartiness, their pink-tinged skin. He hates them. Yet he also feels relieved. Menéndez has admitted defeat.

Whatever happens now, he will not have to fight.

The man with a white mask for a face lies moaning beside him. The screams of the burned are the worst. Their begging is relentless. A man does not have to speak English to understand. But José's hands can barely grip a pencil. His feet—already he has lost a toe. By next summer he might lose a limb. It all depends—cold is a slow thief.

That evening José bends down, looks at the floor. Beneath the end of the cot, in the dust, a photograph lies face down. He stretches out his numb fingers and slides the snapshot forward. It is not what he expects. A boy and a girl, brother and sister maybe, in front of a house with open French doors. The children's hair is uneven, cut by a careless hand. The girl has lighter hair and a pointier chin. She is squinting, looking slightly to the left, not directly at the photographer, but past him. Her swimsuit is ruched, a froth of fabric. The boy beside her looks straight at the camera. His trunks are white. He is perhaps eleven: skinny, pale, a boy who cannot imagine being a man.

Behind the children, a woman sits reading intently while a toddler with curly hair stares at something beyond the frame. Nothing is written on the back: no names or date. The picture is adrift; there is no reason for José to keep it. He almost lets it go. But instead, he stuffs it up his sleeve.

An eye for an eye.

"You are lucky," says the doctor in Ushuaia, after the POWs have been repatriated, greeted by biscuit-throwing crowds before being herded into a shed. "There is necrosis now in the fingers only. The feet will take another two months before you can safely walk without crutches. The hands a little longer—we must continue to splint them. Your frostbite is the worst I have seen."

José feels a strange relief. The city is just the way it was before his crucifixion—ramshackle and dispirited—but it is now haunted, in flickers, by barefoot men and women, dogs without leashes gnawing on hunks of raw meat. José can see them, crouching over their fires, although no one acknowledges their presence. The returning soldiers crowd toward the fence around the shed, pass their phone numbers over to civilians, beg them to call their families, tell them they are alive.

"What happened?" asks the balding doctor, setting down his clipboard and pen.

"I don't remember."

"Well, something did—I can see from the scars."

"I was bayonetted."

"Yes. And…"

José opens his mouth and then closes it. He should know better. This is a test, and he isn't going to fail.

"War," says José, shrugging.

The doctor nods. José is helped into a chair and wheeled away.

Later he is taken in a convoy to Buenos Aires. He is hospitalized. He stays for nine weeks. During that time, military personnel come to interview him. They make him sign an agreement that he will not talk about what happened.

"Your father..." murmurs one of his interrogators, the younger lieutenant with a moustache. "Wasn't he an intellectual?"

"Is," says José.

The lieutenant kicks him in the foot. José feels the splint bite into his skin.

His companion nods. For a moment José is convinced he has seen him before—a thickset man of few words, balding on top, with an unmistakable swagger. The pain in his foot makes it impossible to think.

According to the rumours, democracy is coming. Thatcher has won. In Britain, she has become a hero. Wonder Woman. The Iron Lady: made of tougher stuff than the Belgrano.

The right middle finger is gone. José wonders when he will draw again, looks at his remaining fingers, jutting out of their splints, blistered and dry. Already he can move them more easily. His doctors say he is making a remarkable recovery. Hopefully he will not lose any more.

There are other soldiers in the hospital, most with much worse injuries than his. Another is also recovering from frostbite, but they do not talk, just nod from the entrances of rooms. The sun burns outside, ripens the grapes, tans the skins of sunbathers. Yet José refuses to feel it. He nurses his body in the shadows, learns to light each cigarette while barely holding on, makes loose sketches in ballpoint pen on the backs of envelopes and pages from magazines.

He does not want to see his mother, tells her over the telephone not to come. He will see her when he is well. It won't be long. His voice trembles. He finds it difficult to talk. It's as if he has swallowed the wolf—he feels it rise in him every time he opens his mouth. Soon I will grow fur on my hands, he thinks. The wolf in him is a knot of wet hair he can't swallow and is a reason not to speak. At night, he wakes and returns to the snow, arms and legs stretched out across the bed. The sound of trolleys is the sound of shells, rumbling along corridors full of helmets laid down in surrender, with no truce in sight. During the day, he works on his recovery, the line that connected him to his father almost erased now, a faint indentation on a blank page.

One afternoon, waking from a dream, he sees a man who resembles Carlos, but who carries himself like a petty bureaucrat, strutting along the hallway, hand in hand with a man who resembles Vargas. "We must find a way to make him repay his debts," announces the bureaucrat, glancing in at José, who closes his eyes quickly. "He owes us, after all."

Vargas nods, his large teeth too big for his shrunken mouth.

When José is finally released, he takes the bus home to his mother's apartment. His key still fits. Inside is silence and dust. His footsteps echo as he enters the living room. Most of his father's books have disappeared. His mother returns soon after he arrives, drops her bags when she sees him in the hallway, and runs to kiss him. Her hair, he notices, is now threaded with grey. She is wearing dark glasses. When she takes them off, her eyes are ringed with shadow.

"You do not look like yourself," she says.

"No." *I am Carlos's ghost,* he thinks.

"We thought you were winning," she says. "They told us you

were winning."

They embrace again, Rosa kissing José's neck, pulling at his hair. José grips Rosa's shoulders, her red gabardine jacket, wishes she would let him go, aware that his nerves are now dead, that he cannot feel.

"Let me make you something to eat," says Rosa.

"I will sleep in my old room."

"José..." begins his mother, her voice thick.

"Please don't ask me anything."

He goes into his room and drops his kit bag on the bed. His hand throbs. His old school books still sit on the shelf below his Serú Girán posters, an old model car, and his art materials: a cigar box of pencils, a blackened stub of eraser, an aluminum sharpener. He opens his atlas to see if the portrait of Gaby is still there. Yes.

Perhaps he should go and visit her. But she is likely busy. She has a job. He has heard she is getting married. They say it will be a new, democratic Argentina—already the president is in hiding, ashamed to show his face.

He has not kept any sketches from the hospital. He ripped them up on the last day and, afraid he'd set off the fire alarm, burned them by the handful in a glass ashtray beside an open window. His sketches were of the nurses, pieces of furniture, cups, flower vases: objects without political or philosophical weight. Once, he had attempted to draw a donkey, but its eye was so mournful he had to erase it. Now that his hands are less his own, he has to accept that his lines will be less assured. He will draw with precision, not the faith of a blind man. Every abandoned line an unanswerable question. Back and forth like a weaver undoing knots.

His mother has turned on the radio and is frying meat and onions, garlic and tomatoes. José's mouth waters; so do his eyes. He pictures Rosa stirring the food in the frying pan, swaying her hips to the music. Did she keep Carlos's *Iliad*? If she burned it, he will never forgive her.

I am Achilles, he remembers. *I am immortal.* He can walk now, with the slight hint of a limp. He can write, draw, light and extinguish a cigarette, masturbate, feed himself, wipe his own ass, and even sign his own name on a cheque if necessary. Like Jesus Christ, he lives again, but not at his father's right hand.

He takes down the cigar box and opens it, selects a blue stub of 2B and sharpens it. Then he tears a sheet of blank paper out of his sketchbook and places it on top of the atlas, shakes out his hand and tries his best to relax it.

A dog howls. A blue Ford Falcon speeds down the street while downstairs Rosa weeps, dances, cooks. They have lost the islands and there's a wolf inside him, but for now the only question is what to draw.

IV

What José draws, the month after he returns from the hospital, is his finger, his amputated right middle finger. He draws it the size of his hand. Using all his pencils, he shades and shapes this portrait until he cannot improve it, and then he sets fire to it until it is ash. He burns it in a casserole dish in his mother's kitchen, then tips the ash into the garbage can. This is his funeral for his finger, the missing manhood Miguel joked about before they parted ways in the POW camp. Then he does the same for his left little toe.

No one talks much about the war. The first thing is to get a job. José tries a few restaurants but soon tires of burning himself. He's a decent cook but there are just too many weapons available in kitchens, especially for a man with numb hands. Instead he gets a position as a night janitor and works in a bookstore during the day.

He reads natural history, travel, science fiction, anything that isn't about the here and now. His boss does not seem to mind. Business is slow. José thinks about Miguel. He even looks up the number of the shoe store, Nuevos Zapatos Italianos. But he cannot call. Instead he filches romance novels, motorcycle magazines.

José wants to move out of his mother's apartment. He

cannot stand Raúl, Rosa's new boyfriend, whom she met in a café during the last months of the war. The old man tries to be kind to him, but he drives José crazy. José does not want or need another father.

Raúl is a good singer. He plays guitar. At night after supper he serenades Rosa and the two grow sentimental together. Sometimes Rosa talks about Carlos, and Raúl does not seem to mind.

Raúl has tattoos. He has done time in jail, Rosa says, but is a pious man. His handwriting is childish, he can barely sign his own name properly. Meanwhile, Carlos's papers lie unread in the other room. Yet Rosa is infatuated. She has put on weight, bought new clothes, has given up searching for answers, and focuses instead on making excellent *pollo a la cubana,* which is Raúl's favourite dish.

Sometimes when his mother is cooking, José stands behind her, panic-stricken at how diminished she seems. Is she shrinking? Her head seems oddly shaped, her thinning, wiry hair now turning white, her scalp visible in places. She is still here, but she isn't the person she was. She is ridiculous, and unaware, a condition that would never be tolerated in the military. He could take her down in an instant. It would take only one blow. His arm twitches.

"Your mother is brave," Raúl says, gravy dripping down his unshaven chin.

It's true that back in the sixties she helped organize a factory strike. The sight of his mother on the shoulders of one of her comrades, yelling slogans, is not one José can ever forget. But he also knows she is afraid.

"Are you grateful or not?" asks Raúl, lifting himself up halfway from the table.

"Shh, let him eat," says Rosa. "You, too: please, just relax."

After too many nights of this, José moves out. He finds

a place with a man named Da Silva, who works out every day at the gym. Da Silva wants to be a professional boxer. He came into the bookstore one day looking for books on weight training, and he and José struck up a conversation. Da Silva also served in the Malvinas. He has a bullet lodged in his calf to prove it. He also has that dead look in his eyes.

⸙

"You draw, chico?" asks Da Silva one night shortly after José arrives with a single suitcase. José's room is extremely small: a closet, really, only big enough for a bed and a tiny desk made from two wooden planks and a pile of bricks. But he is miles away from his mother and Raúl.

His sketchbook is out, as well as his pencils, arranged alongside each other in military fashion. Each is angled precisely, ready for action, across the top of his crude desk.

"Even with the stumps?" Da Silva nods at José's disfigured hands.

José clenches his remaining fingers. "Even with the stumps."

"You should meet my sister," says Da Silva. "She is studying design. Always drawing, always criticizing everything."

"Like what?"

"Posters, billboards, brochures—you name it. She thinks she's something special. She wears designer clothes even though my family cannot afford them. Light-fingered. I've seen her do it. It's amazing what she can lift in a crowded store."

"Well, don't bring her into the bookstore or I'll get fired."

"Oh, Juanita doesn't steal books. Only clothing. Clothing and art supplies. Maybe a little makeup now and again."

Juanita comes over to inspect José the following week, and appraises him coldly.

"You'll do," she says tersely, lighting up a cigarette.

Do for what? wonders José, forcing a smile.

"What's wrong with this?" asks Juanita. She's holding open a three-part brochure about vacation apartments in Balcarce. José isn't interested, but tells her anyway. The type is too small, the photographs blurred, the logo for the company is ugly.

"And what about this?" She holds up a tiny business card. João Benin: Typographer and Graphic Designer.

"Looks okay. Good choice of typeface."

"He's my fiancé," says Juanita. "We're getting married."

Da Silva, sprawled on the couch, cuts in: "He's also her boss."

"We might have a position available for a junior designer, if you are prepared to work hard."

"Are you offering me a job?"

"Of course I am!"

"But I don't have any qualifications."

"It's okay. You have an eye. We can teach you the rest." Juanita glances at her brother. "He told me you were good. Do you want it or not?"

"I guess so," says José, feeling stunned. He'll have to leave the bookstore. He'll have to stop borrowing books. How will he get books now? Maybe he will have to return to the library. The thought gives him shivers. He wonders if he might find his father among the shelves.

"Jesus, listen to him! Talk about ungrateful." Juanita throws up her hands in mock horror. "I offer the boy a job, and he says, 'I guess so.' How do you think you are going to afford the rent? Because it would be a shame to have to toss you out."

Is this a threat? José grins nervously. On the other hand, he does need a change. And learning on the job would be good. He needs graphic skills. "Okay," he says. "All right, I am interested, Juanita. Tell your fiancé I am very grateful. When should I come in for an interview?"

"Tomorrow morning. My brother will bring you over. Nine o'clock sharp, and make sure you are looking handsome. We don't want any down-and-outers in our shop."

❦

The shop itself, located in a nameless plaza in Once, is shabby: a smoke-filled, coffee-stained pigsty with fluorescent lights, a mess of cups and machines sitting on stained beige carpeting. João is hairy, sweaty and boastful, forty years old with three failed businesses behind him. He has just taken over the shop from an elderly Japanese man who died of a heart attack while typesetting brochures for an upscale brothel. These are the clientele João feels comfortable with—people who operate in a netherworld, never ones to do things by the book.

He explains all this quite openly to José. He also explains that he will be putting him on a probationary wage for six months and expects José to learn everything about the business in two weeks so he can hand over several important accounts to him while João and Juanita head off on their honeymoon. José hadn't realized they were getting married quite so soon.

José takes the job. He senses it will distract him from his weariness. Within two weeks he has learned how to operate the Linotype and the halftone camera. He has also mostly become immune to the mess and stink of the place. Only, his eyes hurt more and more.

Da Silva seems pleased. He slaps José on the back and says he knew as soon as he saw him that João and he were going to be friends. José is surprised, does not feel like João's friend. But after nine months of working for João, the agency is flourishing and he has made himself indispensable. It seems there are enough shady businesses in Buenos Aires that need quick turnarounds, cash-in-hand service, with no records kept, no questions asked, that the whole leaky boat can remain afloat. José discovers that he likes no questions asked. He enjoys the pressure and tension that drive him every day, the impossible problems he's required to solve, for which he receives virtually no thanks. Work takes up brain space and leaves him so mentally exhausted that all he can do afterwards is walk and smoke.

His body hurts. His knees, elbows, hands, and feet all ache, and he has strange tingling sensations in his remaining toes and fingers, many of which he cannot fully discern. Once or twice he cuts himself with a layout knife and doesn't even notice until blood is streaming down the light table. Sometimes it's hard to manipulate tiny pieces of type. But he does not tell anyone. He needs the job and that's that. Besides, how could he go to a doctor and ask for treatment without explaining what happened to him? There's an official version, taken down by the military doctors, but he knows he might slip and accidentally say the wrong thing. The more time goes on the more confused he feels. Better to just ignore the aching and needling. All in all, it doesn't seem worth the risk.

He moves out of Da Silva's place and takes a small flat near the Congreso, visits his mother and Raúl every week. He convinces them he is happy, they don't need to worry, although Rosa will keep at him about girls. In his spare time he lifts weights with Da Silva, and on the weekends he works on his own art: faces scribbled out or elongated in horror, the recognizable (Miguel's mouth) ripped apart and reconfigured in mutant forms. Tendrils of frozen fire.

The first time José sees Miguel after the war is at Rosa's. José suggests they meet there, because he is ashamed of his empty apartment. Besides, he'd like Miguel to meet his mother. Rosa is always lamenting José's lack of friends. His old comrade roars up on his motorbike, armed with flowers, a big bunch of yellow roses for Rosa. "Because of your name," he says, breaking into a grin.

After exchanging kisses, Rosa takes the flowers and shows him into the kitchen, where she proceeds to make a chocolate cake while telling him her life story.

She never asks once about the war.

"You're looking pretty good," says Miguel, casually, as he is leaving. "Even without the finger." He smiles, still partially toothless. Rosa has insisted on getting José's teeth fixed.

"When will that boy come again? He's very polite. He doesn't seem much like a soldier."

"He sells shoes."

"Of course." Rosa likes shoes.

José has practiced saying it. "He saved my life."

"Oh." She pauses. "You never told me about that."

A chill goes over him. He rubs his hands together, opens his mouth but the wolf is in his throat.

A few weeks later, Miguel gives José a helmet. Off they ride, out into the suburbs, and then the country, eventually winding up at an old, rundown hotel where, stuck for anything to say, José gets blind drunk and passes out. He wakes before dawn, slumped in an old wicker chair. The grass is wet, and Miguel nowhere to be seen.

According to the wing mirror of the bus he eventually boards alone, he has a black eye. Once home, he stands in the bathroom and weeps.

Where the hell have you been? his mother whispers. José flinches; his mother's voice is full of contempt. *You are not the same, José Ramírez.*

None of them are. They have left one kind of hell for another, an archipelago of shame that remains unmapped. *Cowards, losers.* These were the words that greeted them when they arrived home and slunk separately back into their unfinished lives. Even now José recognizes his comrades not so much from their faces as from their bearing: hunched over, bent from some invisible burden they each wish more than anything to turn away from. He rarely mentions his own military service, except in the company of other veterans, many of whom are drunkards, or apologists, bent on pretending their mission had a purpose; that it was not merely suffering for its own sake. "Tell me again why we went?" he asks these men in his head.

"To prove our might."

"To bring us Bignone."

"To destroy our chances in the World Cup."

"Bullshit," he replies, crushing his cigarette. As far as he is concerned, war has no point, and yet he is obsessed with its questions.

Rosa has remade herself. Why can't he? Her new job is answering the phone for a firm that manufactures medical aids, and she lives in a one-bedroom flat by herself, although Raúl visits her almost every day. It's as if all the trusses, crutches, hoists and artificial limbs at Rosa's work somehow compensate for the physical absence around which Rosa's grief and fury swirl.

They have no physical remains, only Carlos's glasses. Of all his possessions, they are the one item Rosa keeps, beside her bible, polished with a soft cloth. She claims not to believe in God, to still be an atheist, but José sees her cross herself when agitated, when locking the door at night, or in the busy streets.

These days, insists Raúl, life is all about the future. He does not like it when José is gloomy. He says it is time to forgive, to move on. José does his best, and Raúl certainly grills a delicious steak. Meanwhile, Carlos remains silently pressed between books, and the Malvinas travel with José, surrounding him with sharp rocks no one can navigate. *Rescue me,* says his father, whispering up from the headlines of the newspaper. *Don't give up on me.* José strokes the page.

"Your father was married at your age," says Rosa one evening in September. Raúl is out, and she has taken the opportunity to tailor a shirt for him, laying it lovingly across the kitchen table, marked with chalk where its seams need to be moved. "Whatever happened to that nice girl, Gaby? The one you saw a few times after you came back."

José lifts his head from the newspaper he is again not reading. "She's married. Don't you remember? She has a kid now."

"You could too, if you played your cards right." Rosa takes a pin from between her lips, presses it rhythmically in and out of the fabric.

"You need a daughter."

"A daughter-in-law."

"I'm doing my best. I need to get set up first." In fact, finding a wife is the last thing on his mind. It's all he can manage just to get out of bed.

"I never see you with any girls."

"That's because I never bring them home." He remembers the first time he looked in his parents' wardrobe, after Carlos had been gone for over a year. He'd been tempted to try something on, but it felt sacrilegious.

"Why not? Are you ashamed?"

"Ashamed of what—my mother? I don't think so." He looks at her. She meets his gaze.

"Bring someone home. Please, José. Let me cook her a dinner. I will charm her, you will see. I know lots of tasty, sexy recipes…"

"I know you do."

"Are you all right?"

"Yes. Of course." Such lies are José's newest truths.

V

"Did they succeed?"

"What?" Five years have passed, and José and Miguel are in a Montevideo bar, drinking shots of whisky. It's only eleven in the morning and already José feels drunk. This is how it has been for the past five days.

"Did they kill you?"

They are in the old city and tourists are everywhere, but there are even more Uruguayans, for it's Carnaval and the place is crazy. The previous night he and Miguel brought two Spanish girls back to their hotel room and one passed out in the bathroom while the other sat up talking non-stop until Miguel silenced her with his lips and got her into bed with him, at which point José had no choice but to listen. The noise was relentless.

Miguel tries again. "Are you alive? Or should I have left you?"

"Why are you talking about this? You think it's safe to discuss?" José is irritated. His friend talks about the war, or refuses to, at will.

"I am asking how you are doing, my friend. Is that illegal?"

José watches the glittering pasties on the dancer's nipples, and the crazy, peacock-blue headdress waving above her. He watches her bend down and stand up again, like a limbo dancer, shimmying under his nose as he finishes his shot.

"I'm fine," he says.

"Good," says Miguel. But José knows it's not the end of the discussion.

"I will call you when I decide."

"Decide what?"

It's several hours later, and they're lying on their beds. The air is extremely humid, the heat enervating. The wooden fan above their heads reminds José of a helicopter rotor. The motion is nauseating. He has to look at the curtains instead, shifting lightly in the breeze.

"Decide that I've had enough and it's time to die."

José sits up. "What do you mean?" Anger surges through him, turns his muscles rigid. His hands are suddenly fists in his lap.

"I am not a hero. I just happened to find you. Truthfully, I was running away."

"From what?"

Miguel softly taps his head. "I'm afraid of myself, José."

José's mind whirls.

Miguel continues. "If one day I phone you, you must tell my family. That is all I ask. Otherwise, never speak of it. Ever. You understand?"

José nods his head. But he doesn't understand. Little lights shimmer behind his eyes.

That night they both get very drunk and come home without women. José is angry. Why did Miguel invite him? The trip is an impossible luxury for a struggling artist. José would not have come if Miguel hadn't paid. His family does not travel. Neither does Miguel's. Yet somehow José had to come; just as soon as Miguel casually invited him, he knew he had to come.

He told his mother he was going with a group of ambitious designers; women, also. Perhaps he would make connections, toward work or marriage. The whole trip was a lie.

"I hate this fucking place," says Miguel, as the fan whirs above them. He lets out a grunt and punches the wall, and his fist goes through the plaster. José pulls him backward, they fall onto the floor and José punches Miguel, knocks him unconscious.

A woman cries out: there is someone in the hallway, weeping. José opens the door a crack, peers through at a woman in a nightgown.

"I'm sorry," he says. "It's nothing. My friend is just drunk."

She retreats to her room.

"Jesus," mutters José. He thinks of leaving, but what's the use? Lying down next to Miguel, he listens to his friend's breathing.

When he comes to, Miguel seems confused.

"It's cold," he says, shivering visibly. "I'm dying of cold."

"Come on, buddy, we're here in Montevideo."

"Shush. Don't let them find me."

"Here," says José, putting Miguel's arm around his shoulder. "Let's go to sleep. This is too crazy for me." He helps Miguel to his bed then lies down on it also. Miguel has blood trickling out of his mouth: another one of his teeth has broken off. José cleans it gently, fetching a glass of water and a face cloth. Miguel sleeps.

The day passes, and outside another night's festivities start up. Fireworks burst above the city like munitions, followed by explosions of shattered bodies and firecrackers, the shouts of men and women among the beat of music that consists mostly of drums and bass at this remove: all of it covered in snow, suddenly, and veiled by exhaustion, the exhaustion of keeping secrets for too long.

⸙

José is smoking in the office when the call comes.

"Can you speak up?" José puts his finger in his ear.

"Yes—José, it's Miguel. Long time, eh?"

"Indeed." They have not seen each other for six months. Not since Montevideo. José feels his jaw muscles tighten. How did Miguel get hold of his work number? The Rueda proofs are due at 2:30 PM, and it's already 1:47, according to his watch.

"How is your mother?"

"Rosa? She's fine." José's knee jiggles. "Listen, is there…"

"I just wanted to call."

José pauses. "I'm glad you called. But, listen, I have…"

"Busy times."

"Yes."

Miguel's breath buzzes in José's ear. José crushes his cigarette. "Miguel…"

Miguel says something that José can't decipher.

"Sorry?" It's still very difficult to hear.

"I said I have to leave." The phone clicks off. Nausea squeezes José's gut. His ears buzz. Shouldn't Miguel be at work? José looks at his hands, frozen flat on the tabletop. Probably it's nothing. He extinguishes his Camel in an ashtray he hasn't emptied in days. He makes an effort to concentrate on the newspaper headings. According to them, life is better now, Argentina is a democracy and the economy is limping along. Privatization is in vogue, and businesses want new visuals, new brands.

As if in a trance, José takes a knife and cuts around the type, brings it to the waxer and runs it through. Then he pastes it into the ad beneath the black and white diagram of a hexagonal tower built out of plastic triangles connected by hinges. He knows the hinges do not work. They either stick or crack apart. Also, he knows that the inventor has only made ten of them. He is banking on getting lots of orders for Christmas, at which point he will begin making more. Mr. Rueda, your plastic toy is a breakthrough. It will revolutionize childhood in Argentina. No longer will we need to borrow our play things. We'll have a fantastic set that is homegrown. Now, do you mind telling me again what your budget is? No, sir, I am not looking for a handout. I am simply wanting us to remain on the same page. You wish to place an ad. You also want letterhead. Business cards, catalogues, illustrations and instruction manuals are all in your future. It seems to me you should treat me as your friend.

For all José knows, Mr. Rueda will never come back. On the other hand, he could be spending his summer pasting up a mind-numbing catalogue of plastic triangles, each with a tiny label, together with footnotes. He feels his heart pound. He grabs the receiver and dials the shoe store, then Miguel's home number, but there is no answer. Terror flips the breaker and he's up out of his chair, heading out the door and running down the spiral stairwell to the back door, which leads to a stinking alley located between a dubious nightclub and a pharmacy. He takes a deep breath and retches. Rights himself. Shivers. Goes back upstairs and grabs his jacket, tells Juanita he's popping out for a few minutes and will be back by two o'clock.

"What about Rueda?" Juanita crosses and uncrosses her meaty arms.

"If you mean the proofs, they're practically done. All I have to do is typeset the logo."

"Don't make me fire you, Ramírez. I would not enjoy that." Her hair is newly dyed and glisteningly metallic. Perhaps, part of

José's brain intones, Juanita Benin herself is made up of plastic triangles, and Paolo Rueda is coming to finally disassemble her. His appointment with José is just a ploy. If so, José is clearly doing Rueda a favour in refusing to complete the proofs entirely on time, for this will give Rueda more reason to speak with Juanita, to slip his hand up the back of her blouse and open up her vinyl packaging.

"Ramírez? Can you hear me?"

"Yes, Benin."

"Ramírez, are you ill?"

"No, Benin."

"Well then?"

"I'll see you very soon."

José hooks his jacket over one shoulder and as soon as he reaches the alley he starts running. Soon he is at the subway. He slumps against a window, feeling exhausted. He'd never be accepted into the military these days. The mere sight of a hospital makes him afraid. He often changes his route through the city to avoid them. He detests public spaces in general and he never, ever visits his mother at work.

Hold on my friend, he murmurs. *Hold on, I'm coming.* A sad-looking man gets on at Peru stop and starts playing Beatles tunes badly on a battered guitar. PROUD VETERAN, says a sticker on his backpack. José turns away.

When José arrives at the shoe store, bookended by a tiny bakery and a rundown *kiosco,* it looks empty. But the sign on the door says OPEN.

"Hello?"

The door swings. The lights aren't on, but the store is bright.

"Hello?" he calls into the back room.

The place smells of glue. The racks are full, but the shoes on display look dusty and damaged, except for the ones in the window. White high-heeled pumps, brown suede loafers. Gold tango sandals, barely used.

A pen and notebook sit on the desk beside a battery-powered calculator. Behind the desk, tins of shoe polish are piled on shelves.

"Miguel?"

Since their father died, six months after the war, Miguel and his sisters have kept the store running between them. Miguel's younger sister, Vicky, desperately wants to move to America. She thinks if she goes to Los Angeles she will be discovered and end up in a movie or one of the soap operas. She's crazy about Madonna and still wears the kind of chunky jewellery and fingerless lace gloves the singer wore in *Desperately Seeking Susan.* Miguel's older sister, Inés, is the opposite. Religious and devoted to her parents, she despairs over the books and is constantly trying to revamp the store to improve it. Once, she even set up a shelving unit to display bibles, and she hung rosaries on hooks beside the till. Surprisingly this was quite a success with the older women who shopped there. But Miguel wouldn't stand for it. He demanded she get rid of the bibles or else he would quit. These days Inés is absent, running a church school in one of the provinces with her new husband, a zealous preacher. Vicky, too, is away at school, so it's Miguel who keeps the place running. José wishes he had listened more closely the few times he'd been here previously.

He pushes through a beaded curtain into the office, where boxes are stacked up in dangerous piles. A kettle sits on the floor beside a cold cup of maté.

"Miguel? Are you here?"

A radio is playing. José turns it off. He glances at his watch: 2:27. Three minutes left for him to finish the Rueda proofs. Juanita will be flexing her arms, ready to engage in hand-to-hand combat. What time did Miguel call? Sweat is slick on José's forehead. He wipes it away with the back of his hand, then looks around for a key, or a sign. There are none. The key he remembers is kept on a hook behind the door of the bathroom. He finds it and locks up.

Bárbara, Miguel's favourite girl, works out of a hotel in the Microcentro. A thirty-five-year-old who looks twenty-two. Miguel often gives her money, even though he knows she spends it on dope. For an addict, she is immaculate—witty and polite, dressed in signature black with bleached blond hair. Bárbara injects herself with heroin daily. She is very smart and likes to read Sartre. Miguel told him this on their way to Montevideo. At that time, he had just met her. Ordinary girls bored him, he'd said, although he still liked boys. Once in a while he would spend a night with one and it was his routine to visit a female prostitute afterwards.

Miguel: six-foot-three, 170 pounds, brown curly hair and a fetish for fancy cologne. Miguel, who, according to his sisters, could never keep his written words on the lines or add up his equations without cheating, but radiated intelligence. He had a spark that helped him through training, a charm and an insolence. Miguel could never stand to see other men punished, yet he could fight like a banshee, without mercy, when the time came and he was up against it. José watched him kill a man, a Brit who had already been shot in the leg. This was a war crime of sorts, but nobody cares now. The one rule Miguel has is that they never talk about it, any of it, ever. Unless he wants to.

José arrives at the hotel where he paces frantically. It's hot outside and the air conditioning is broken. The man at the desk has fallen asleep and José does not have the heart to wake him. Instead he reaches over and carefully takes the key to Bárbara's room from the slot where it lives behind the sleeping man's head. Perhaps Bárbara doesn't live here anymore. But he has to try. He takes the key and quietly moves to the elevator.

She must be out, otherwise her key would not be there. She always leaves it in the slot, in case someone wishes to get into her room. She has a few clients who come and go. Regulars, like Miguel. José's hands are shaking. The key rattles despite his attempts to keep it still. Probably it is nothing. Why would it be nothing? If it is, he will put an end to it.

"Bárbara?"

Piles of clothes, neatly folded, on a green brocade couch. Cigarette butts. Cold coffee. A half-eaten pastry. José's eyes dart. Telephone receiver. Carpet. Stain. Sweet metal stench. Battered shoe, long thin torso.

Blood on the wall.

Back out into corridor. Close the door. Lock it. Unlock it. Open it. Darkness. Winds roar.

The hotel clerk, mouth open. Then the police, guns poised, and the police station. José's fingers, gnarled, around a coffee cup. What was your relationship to the deceased? What were you doing there? *He was a veteran.* José's observation goes unremarked. Miguel's fingerprints found on the pistol, a Glock semi-automatic, the small arms of an officer. *Well done, my friend.* The suicide of a shoe seller in the hotel room of a high-class call girl is only mildly interesting. The newspapers will cover it for a while then the story will be dropped.

VI

"He left no note," says José.

"He must have." Bárbara's voice is hoarse.

"Well, if he did, I didn't find it."

"Did you look?"

"Of course I did. So did the police, and the hotel clerk, and the hotel manager."

Miguel's mother has clawed at him with her hands. Inés screamed over the telephone. Vicky begged, hanging onto his arm. But he has no comfort to give them, only a story he tells until he throws up.

Bárbara is insistent. "But why did he do it? Why? It wasn't the store."

"No, it wasn't the store." José shrugs. This ignorance is a lie, like everything else. The warrah scratches inside his throat.

"He was crazy about you," adds Bárbara. "He once told me he thought of you as his brother."

José had been researching the flora and fauna of the Malvinas, building up a portfolio of drawings. He'd been planning to show someone—Miguel—but now the ashes of the ignited artworks are in a tobacco tin in his sock drawer. Letting the receiver slide from his ear, he retrieves the tin, opens the lid, dips his finger in, to see how they taste. Bitter.

"... and he didn't keep up with his friends. He was always having pretend phone conversations with friends from university who were all still in touch and planning different business ventures. Or saying he had to go and meet so-and-so for a date, but I knew it was all made up. He was a loner. He knew only how to proposition."

"We were in the army together."

"I know."

"Did he say anything about that?"

"Just that you were both young and stupid, and also that you didn't get enough to eat."

Bárbara is not one to sentimentalize. She has lost many friends to AIDS and overdoses.

"Listen, José. I gave him the key because I knew he wouldn't abuse it, and because he needed somewhere to go when things got crazy."

"You also gave him dope."

"He bought his own."

"But he'd shoot up with you."

"Sometimes. But I did not corrupt him. He only got high for a few weeks at a time then he'd quit. He was unusual that way. He could just stop. He had his secrets."

⸙

The truth is, Miguel did leave a note. A faded picture postcard of the Congreso tucked into a scalloped yellow envelope he slid under the phone in Bárbara's room. Before the police arrived, José pocketed it. The doodle on the back was either a map or a diagram, or possibly a design for a new shoe. Wordless and colourless, José knew the drawing was meant for him.

ℵ

Rueda is angry. He throws a cup of coffee at Juanita and storms out of their final meeting, refusing to pay. Juanita tells José not to show his face in the office again. She packs his belongings in a small cardboard box and leaves them outside the back door for him to collect and mails him his last pitiful cheque. But at least she does not scream at him. She does that much.

"My brother was in the war," she says by way of explanation. "And I think that's why he ended up divorced." Nevertheless, she would cut him no slack for losing a client.

"At least he's not dead," says José. Juanita turns away. It's as intimate as they would ever be.

Three weeks after his dismissal from the ad agency, on the four-week anniversary of Miguel's suicide, Rosa has José for dinner. He has told her very little about what happened. Just that a friend passed away.

"Someone from your university cohort?" asks his mother.

José shrugs ambiguously.

"That's terrible! What happened?"

"He hanged himself," says José. His fork, twisting up strands of pasta, is the fan in Montevideo, turning.

"Oh my God," says Rosa, blanching. She sits down.

José twirls and twirls his fork. It is a blade, cutting through air. It is a bayonet. "I'm going away for a little while. It's to do with work." That useful four-letter word.

"Oh, where to?"

"Down south." José is making this up as he goes along.

Rosa's eyebrows arch.

"We're looking to expand our horizons. See if there are possibilities for satellite offices."

Rosa reaches for his hand. She doesn't believe him, but

blessedly does not press him.

"Don't stay away too long, my son." Her grip is painful. José stands. He drops the fork.

"I have to get going, Mami. I'm sorry." He grabs his jacket and runs out the door and doesn't stop until he reaches his own place. It's drab and undecorated, filled with art magazines, a sorry little room he's happy to leave whenever he goes to work. No more of that now. It's impossible to travel to the Malvinas. Nevertheless, he can get close, to the barren, windswept tail end of this fucked-over continent. He has just enough money to pay the fare and tide him over for a week or two of travel before he is destitute. Just like five years ago. It seems right.

A voice has been speaking to him of late, a strange, lilting, European-inflected voice. Just out of earshot, then right at his shoulder. A waft of whisky breath and cigarette smoke with just a hint of the sea and burning flesh. *Are you a coward?* it asks. *Are you?*

Around midnight, Vicky calls. Over the past couple of weeks, she has taken to phoning him after dinner, a few glasses of wine into her grief. "José," she begins. José closes his eyes. He knows what's coming. "I know you were close. What do you think my brother really wanted?"

"To be left alone," says José.

"Was he gay?"

José pauses. "I think so. Yes."

"Did he have a lover?"

"I don't know. We hadn't seen each other in a while." José lifts the receiver away from his ear, then puts it back. Vicky is talking.

"Mama is going crazy. Inés blames the devil. I was saving up for America but now I don't know—how can I leave them like this? I'm angry at him. Why couldn't he tell us something was wrong?"

"It's okay to be angry. I was angry when my father disappeared." José listens to himself: so calm, so reasonable. Did Miguel ever tell his sisters about them?

"Have you learned anything more?" Vicky sounds increasingly agitated.

"No." *Only that he was in a war.*

"I'm sorry. Listen—are you busy tonight?"

Whisky and cigarette smoke. "Yes—no—I'm going on a trip. I'll call you when I get back. You were his favourite sister," he improvises, already making a list of what to take. "Don't forget that."

Vicky cries for a while. José listens until she hangs up.

VII

His name is Carlos Ramírez, and if he closes his eyes he can still see his office the way he left it. His latest hardcover ledger is open, his uncapped fountain pen lies on the desk, spilling blue-black ink across the wood. Behind it, a book, supported by the lectern he built, held open by brass clasps. The chair pushed back, a blue sweater crumpled against its seat, the orderly bookcases to either side, not yet rifled through. On the low table beside the desk, a framed photograph of Rosa, black hair spiralling out of her head scarf, the photograph he took the day they first went swimming together, when she jumped on his back and he took her thighs in his hands. Beside it, one of Josito's drawings, a green cow with purple horns. Inside his heart, an image of Cristina, her blond ponytail swinging as she walks right past him on the street, pretending not to know him, pretending they are not about to meet for wine. How much he wanted her. How he imagined her face.

The documents, he knows, are already safe in Chile, smuggled over the border from Argentina inside pallets of ripening pears. It is his heart he worries about. The shame he feels at the way his body responded to the caresses of his guard. He knew she was detested by the female prisoners, who screamed her name from their cells whenever she passed. Yet for him, just her eyes could rescue him from suffering in those moments when the pain became too much. When it was her turn to beat him, she would direct her blows toward the toughest parts of his torso and avoid his organs. She did not show it, but he knew she cared.

And this knowledge, too, is unbearable.

His name is Carlos Ramírez. He is Carlos Ramírez and he is being transferred somewhere down south. Which is why, now, he uses his customary discipline, systematically visualizes each item inside his abandoned briefcase: two sharpened pencils, packet of blue-black ink cartridges, a calculator, keys. Anything to prevent his mind from wandering, in case it returns to her, the guard with the wooden bat, standing over him as she beats him. Returns to the velvet softness inside her eyes.

Dear Father,

There is an animal in my heart.

Do you remember the time you left me in the library? There was a book that kept me company. An iceberg floated on its cover, in blue-black water. It had large black letters and made a cracking sound as I opened it. It was one of my favourite books, mostly because of the penguins, big as children. In particular, there was a photograph of an adult brooding a downy chick between its legs. The baby was asleep, even though it was very cold. I wanted to be that chick, squished protectively between you and Mother.

After the penguins, I looked at the whales, slippery mammoths that plunged, spouted and plumed. Their backs reminded me of land masses. Did you know the continents have not always been the same? Laurentia, Baltica, Gondwana: I discovered those names in a different book, one about geology, several shelves over. Perhaps you know I was hungry for answers. I liked to marvel, as everyone does, at the Blue Whale, sitting at the top of the pyramid of living whales like a giant torpedo. I was struck in the middle of my chest by longing: that I was so very small was both reassuring and bewildering. I would picture each whale in turn, in descending order of size, calculate how many fathers or fathoms long each one was, until I came to the picture of the tiny human. Just a speck. Could he be you? I would turn the page hurriedly. Then I would study the maps, the historical diagrams of the continent that lies at the bottom of the Earth. Antarctica: a mysterious land, from which people in the past believed a portal opened into the centre of our planet.

At the end of this book there was a section about the Malvinas, and the one mammal that lived there when the islands were discovered by Europeans. The only native mammal was a kind of dog. The illustration of this creature was a meticulous drawing executed in pen and ink, tinted with colour wash. How beautiful it was! And how odd. The animal's head was strangely narrow, and its sharp teeth seemed wrong. How could such a friendly looking creature be fierce? But of course, appearances can be deceiving.

I copied it obsessively, as I did Darwin's drawing of the dodo. To this day I remain entranced by what you would call the poetics of loss. The extinct: how they sometimes seem like gods, and sometimes like clowns, a sorry vestigial that lacks ambition, reflecting back to us our own peculiarity. This wolf-dog, I read, was named the warrah, and died out rapidly when Europeans landed and introduced sheep. Back then I believed the sheep had killed it. But now I understand that the Europeans hunted it, shooting it when it came to their farms. Their guns killed the warrah, along with the Fuegians, who visited the Malvinas in their canoes, with these wolf-dogs as hunting companions.

The warrah lives inside me, Father. I feel it gnawing on my heart. It runs in place in the snow, asks Why? Why? Whenever I think about dying, its scream gathers at the back of my throat.

I dream about going back to the Malvinas, where the animal jumped in, to let it tear its way out. But that place is forbidden to us. All I could do is travel to the southern city of Ushuaia and swim out across the unpredictable currents.

A teenaged boy, a self-styled naturalist, recently unearthed the bones of a warrah while on vacation at the family farm. Curious, he returned to the place several times to dig out pieces of skull, jaw and teeth, and also the bones of its prey. He carried them back to Stanley, where they are being analyzed, carbon dated. I fear they will find my blood on the animal's incisors. I distinctly remember the feel of its teeth.

Am I extinct?

Dear Father, I am now very close to the Southern Ocean. Specifically, I have taken the bus to Ushuaia from Buenos Aires. I was fired from my job at the agency. If I make it back, I will tell Mother the truth.

Father, you have been gone too long. You have become my Odysseus, that ancient hero to whom you devoted your life. I cannot precisely remember your face. The photograph of the three of us that sits on Mother's side table shows a young man with sideburns and thick-rimmed glasses, grinning as he hugs a young woman in a short dress. Where am I? Sitting on a rug, a solemn-faced Buddha. With such carefree parents, who can be surprised by the scowl on my face? Someone had to take suffering seriously. Your hair is thinning. You sweep it back over your tiny bald patch. You do not keep secrets. That is apparent from the clear look in your eyes.

I am alone here at the tip of the continent with only a change of clothes, my sketchbook and pencils, and a pair of old hiking boots. You and I are going to climb the Martial Glacier, and we are taking Miguel. He's dead, you see, and he thinks he won't make it, but I know he will. You are going to carry us half the way. The rest of the way I will carry the two of you—for that is how it goes between a father and son, between friends. We will climb the glacier and when we reach the top, we will release our burdens and fly over the Beagle Channel and find our way to the warrah's home territory, where we will land softly on two or four feet.

Perhaps we will land in the past. Perhaps we will change history ever so slightly, so that only the Yagán ever inhabit the Malvinas. We will invent for ourselves a new, parallel archipelago: The Here-and-Gone Isles. On one of its islands (the rest will be kept as a reserve), the Spanish and English will be invited to set up a colony, to farm the domestic animals they know from home. They will farm until there's no grass left. Meanwhile, we will render their bays unnavigable. No boats will land. The colonizers will eat each other.

The Here-and-Gone Isles will be presided over by penguins and whales. The warrah will flourish there, and outlive us, as we humans kill each other off.

José takes a layout knife and cuts himself with it. Six small incisions, along the inside of his thigh. Blood surfaces. There's a word for what he wants, but he must not speak it. His hands shake. He blots the cuts. All he can think of is fire.

On went Achilles: as a devouring conflagration rages through the valleys of a parched mountain height, and the thick forest blazes, while the wind rolls the flames to all sides in riotous confusion, so he stormed over the field like a fury, driving all before him, and killing until the earth was a river of blood.

VIII

At first, José pretends he is there for no particular reason. You can act like a tourist but still feel like a corpse. You can walk between the hotels and shops and contemplate that you are at *el fin del mundo.* There are ski hills and hiking trails. There are views and postcards and souvenirs. There is also the cold, sending blood back to the core, the ongoing struggle to stay alive.

He distracts himself by reading about Darwin. The man from England who came here on a voyage and encountered the Yagán, who copied the Yagán's every movement. Was it like looking in a mirror?

> *These poor wretches were stunted in their growth, their hideous faces bedaubed with white paint, their skins filthy and greasy, their hair entangled, their voices discordant, and their gestures violent. Viewing such men, one can hardly make oneself believe they are fellow-creatures, and inhabitants of the same world.*

He gave them red cloth. Later most of them died from disease or gunshots. Today José walks on their graves. It is sunny and bright. A red-glowing April morning, unusually clear, the end of the world tipping toward darkness. The Beagle Channel glows.

The houses are blue, yellow, and pink. A single line of smoke rising up.

One night, after he has been here for two weeks, José decides it is the day to climb the glacier. Just a trial run, a little reconnaissance mission. He purchases a fold-out map which outlines the route. He also purchases an apple, shipped here from New Zealand, and a couple of beef empanadas.

Miguel is in his backpack. Although he did not leave any specific instructions, Vicky was convinced her brother wanted to be cremated.

"Don't let me rot in the ground—that's all I'm asking," he said, just once.

Perhaps it was because Miguel had seen so many bodies during the war and knew what decomposition looked like. Vicky arranged the cremation, and José asked for some ashes.

"I'd like to scatter them at sea. In the Southern Ocean."

The funeral home had sold them a beautiful urn, pearly-white with a tight-fitting lid, in which to keep him. José laughed awkwardly as Vicky handled the spoon, the fine smoke-like ash getting in their eyes and making them cough as she poured some of the ashes into a plastic baggie.

José has that baggie in his backpack, along with a box of pencils and the empanadas. He has already sprinkled a portion into the sea. The beach was beautiful and deserted and the ash sank into the green without protest. Today his mission is to visit the cold. He wishes his father could be here too, and José did bring Carlos's copy of the *Iliad,* which is almost the same. It's the only one of his books José has kept, besides the Joyce. To Carlos, those were the bookends of civilization. The *Iliad* goes everywhere with him. The spine is a flap, a piece of loose skin. The back cover is missing completely, and the front is ripped, but still clinging on.

José also brought the photograph. The one of the boy and girl in their swimsuits. It, too, has swelled with meaning. The sunlight of the day radiates out. As if he could be warmed by it. What were their names?

Somewhere in the world there is a photograph of him, lying on the ground, clothed in a filthy uniform, nearly unrecognizable. A picture of an enemy in retreat. José likes to think that as long as he keeps this snapshot of the children, refuses to lose it, that the photograph of him will not disappear either. Because he knows they are linked together. After all, he found it beside the photographer's bed. Perhaps one day there will be an exchange of prisoners. And on that day he will find the man who took his picture and give this one to him: an English childhood, framed in white. For now, its innocence belongs to him.

Dear Mother, Please do not hate me for this; they say on the other side the view is magnificent. Continue as you are. Tap your foot to Raúl's howling, massage his hairy back and laugh at the parakeets in the trees. The war I was conscripted to continues. It's the same war Carlos fought. It never ends. We must battle to save ourselves.

José Ramírez: Notes Toward a Catalogue

1985-1987: FROSTBITE SERIES (Figure 1)
A series of drawings revealing the effects of severe frostbite on a healthy man's extremities, utilizing anatomical illustration techniques and impressionistic mapping; pen and ink, pencil, chalk, gouache and charcoal.

1987-1990: GUNSHOT WOUND SERIES (Figure 2)
A series of drawings examining paths of bullets through the

human body and the damage inflicted on surrounding tissues, drawn in pen and ink, pencil, chalk, charcoal and collage.

1989-1993: OTHER WOMEN SERIES (Figure 3)
A series of occasional drawings of female models, alongside, and occasionally hybridized with, drawings of animals: women with the heads of zebras, women with the bodies of deer, etc., chalk, charcoal, pencil, collage, gouache.

1992-1997: QUIXOTE SERIES (Figure 4)
Based on the story of Don Quixote, featuring knights and soldiers on the backs of animals and insects, often in absurd combinations, e.g. British paratroopers on the backs of ants; pen and ink, pencil, graphite, collage.

1994-1998: MAP SERIES (Figure 5)
Drawings incorporating fragments of maps, real and imaginary, often replacing real place names with imagined ones, or maps of seemingly incompatible places collapsed into one, e.g. map of the surface of the moon merged with map of roadside attractions in the state of Arizona; collage, pencil, pen and ink, mixed media. Or perhaps, instead, a defining performance piece entitled THE GLACIER, for which he would only require rope, pegs, assorted personal amulets, and minimal clothing. A small canvas backpack containing two books, a photograph (Figure 6), and an enigmatic doodle of unknown origin (Figure 7).

Gaby had been shocked when she last saw José, only the second time since the war. The first time was a month after his return. José had asked her parents where she lived. He was drunk and they could smell it. José got angry and kicked a dent in their front door. The next day Gaby phoned and asked him to meet her. She said her parents would kill her if they knew—as would her fiancé. The café was easy to find. There she was: his heart fluttered. It was hard not to smile. She looked the same, except with streaked blond hair. She was also wearing an expensive-looking watch and high-heeled shoes.

José ordered an espresso. She ordered Perrier.

"You look good," José said.

"So do you," Gaby lied, her eyes wide with shock at his unkempt appearance.

José leaned over and tried to kiss her but she withdrew.

Gaby studied José's fingers. The missing one called out to him from wherever it had gone: the medical waste bin, likely.

"You survived," said Gaby.

"I killed a man," said José. "Men."

She had tears in her eyes.

The second time they met was only a year ago. Gaby was divorced by then. José avoided mentioning this, tempting though it was, for he knew she also had a little boy, and despite the country's advances there was still shame in that. He imagined her son: an innocent with her eyes. My God, how would she care for him? Rosa said she would manage.

"Her parents will come around. You will see. No one wants to pass up a chance to know their grandchildren."

José had bumped into Gaby outside her lawyer's office, the day after Miguel killed himself. He had been overwrought. He had not slept. He had not shaved. He had spent the night drinking, wandering the streets. Miguel's family had invited him in but he felt like an intruder. There was a madness in him. He phoned Juanita, told her he would not be in. He could have worked, but something in his mind had turned off and he could no longer pretend. He tripped over himself. Gaby had called his name.

"José?"

He stopped.

"Is that you, Gaby?" He no longer knew what to believe.

She smiled. It was definitely Gaby. She looked tired. She was wearing glasses. She also looked skinny. She was no longer beautiful. He reached out and pulled her close, sobbed into her shoulder.

"My friend just killed himself."

Gaby rubbed his back, as if he were a child. But when a couple slipped past, also leaving the lawyer's office, she abruptly pushed him away. Her eyes were wide. She was afraid.

José saw her glance at his maimed fingers.

"I don't know what to do. I'm just walking the streets."

"I should go. My son is waiting for me. He is at my parents'. I'm sorry, José." She turned, swinging her large leather purse over her shoulder, and he understood then that their lives had finally separated. She was in her adult world and he was in his.

Once upon a time, many thousands of years ago, the people gathered near Ushuaia to hold a grand meeting. And it was at this meeting that the men finally gained control, for up until that time the women were in charge of society because of their superior paddling skills and considerable magic. You can still visit this place, if you wish. It is a place of power. It is also, in some ways, a place of grief.

The world is brown and white, the silence around him absolute.

The tourists have gone. Most of them do not come up here to the top of the mountain, to the edge of the glacier. Those who do stay only long enough to take a few snapshots then head back down to Ushuaia for food and warmth. José wanders around, taking in the views: the forest, the mountains, and in the distance the blue of the ocean, suspended below the horizon like a dream.

The sun is going down, the temperature falling. He feels pain in all the familiar places: the absences, the phantom limbs. He has brought his rope as well as his stakes, whittled from tree branches he collected earlier. He has brought a mallet to drive them deep into the frozen ground as fast as possible. He has worn thin clothing, as useless as the uniform they gave him all those years ago. He has decided not to eat, so he will have less reserve. The empanadas are an offering.

He takes out the rope and ties it around his ankles then ties the other end to the first stake. Nice and tight. He doesn't want to be able to pull himself free. Next, he attempts the difficult part: tying the ropes around the stakes and around his wrists. He's practiced this several times down in the hostel, as well as for a week or two back home before he left. He thought he had it down. But up here it's more difficult. The cold is getting into his fingers, already compromising his effort. He cannot feel properly. He cannot feel.

He has lain the photograph, the doodle, and the *Iliad* beside him. Whoever finds him will have a puzzle to solve. Collage is collision: the friction created between objects that may or may not have any connection to each other. The mind makes meaning, even where there is none.

⸙

Where are you, warrah? I'm lying here, dreaming of you running.

Fuck, it's cold. And so beautiful.

⸙

A sharp tooth presses into his neck. He shudders. If only he could keep still and let the cold settle in. He thinks of Charles Darwin, the pieces of truth he stole from this place: live finches, an ancient tortoise, the eyes of an Arctic fox preserved in red wine.

Dear Father, I know too much.

The shuddering stops. He smells stale cigarette smoke, corpses. Death places its heavy canvas across him.

⸙

Something takes the back of his skull in its jaws, shakes him hard. *Miguel,* he begs. *Stop running. Papi, too. Tell me I am a man.* Shakes him harder, until he gives up, wrestles the stakes from the ground and stands, vertiginous. The glacier glows. Patient. Just where he left it.

He picks up the puzzle.

It is the journey back down into civilization that proves to be the hardest. The knowledge that he cannot even die.

FIGURES

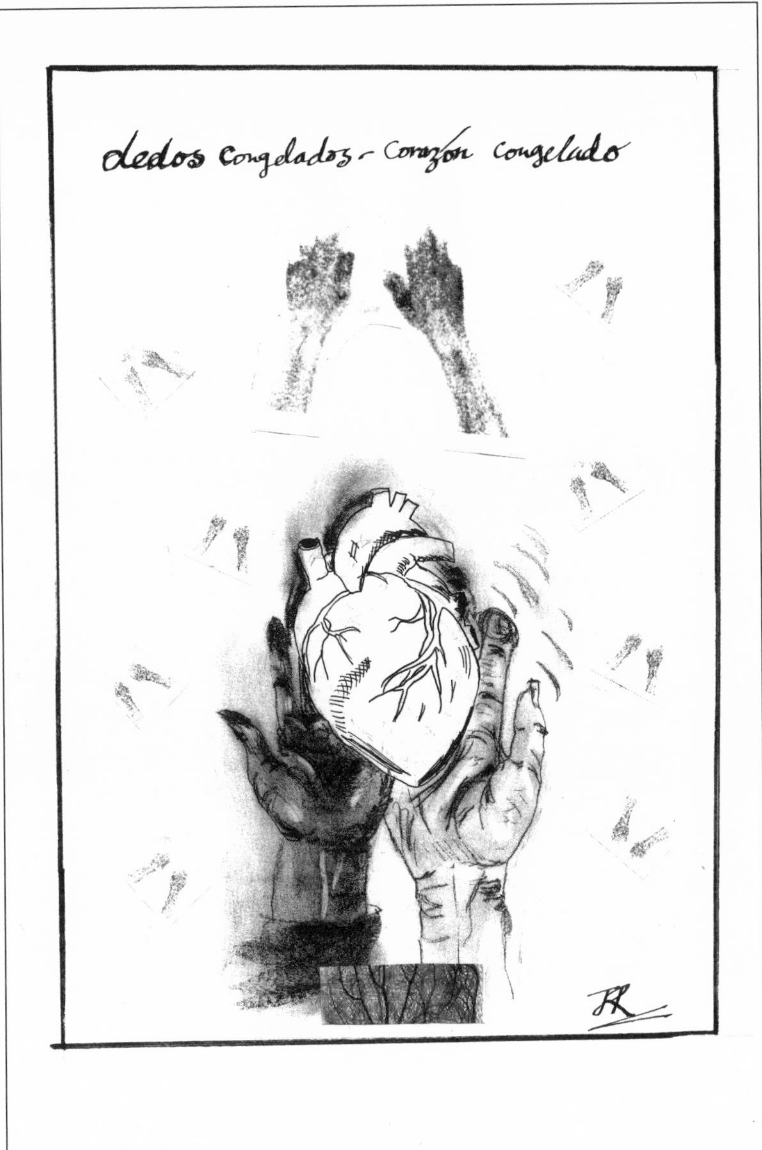

FIGURE 1: *José Ramírez, 1986.* Dedos congelados, corazón congelado *(preliminary sketch); pen and ink, collage, chalk and pencil.*

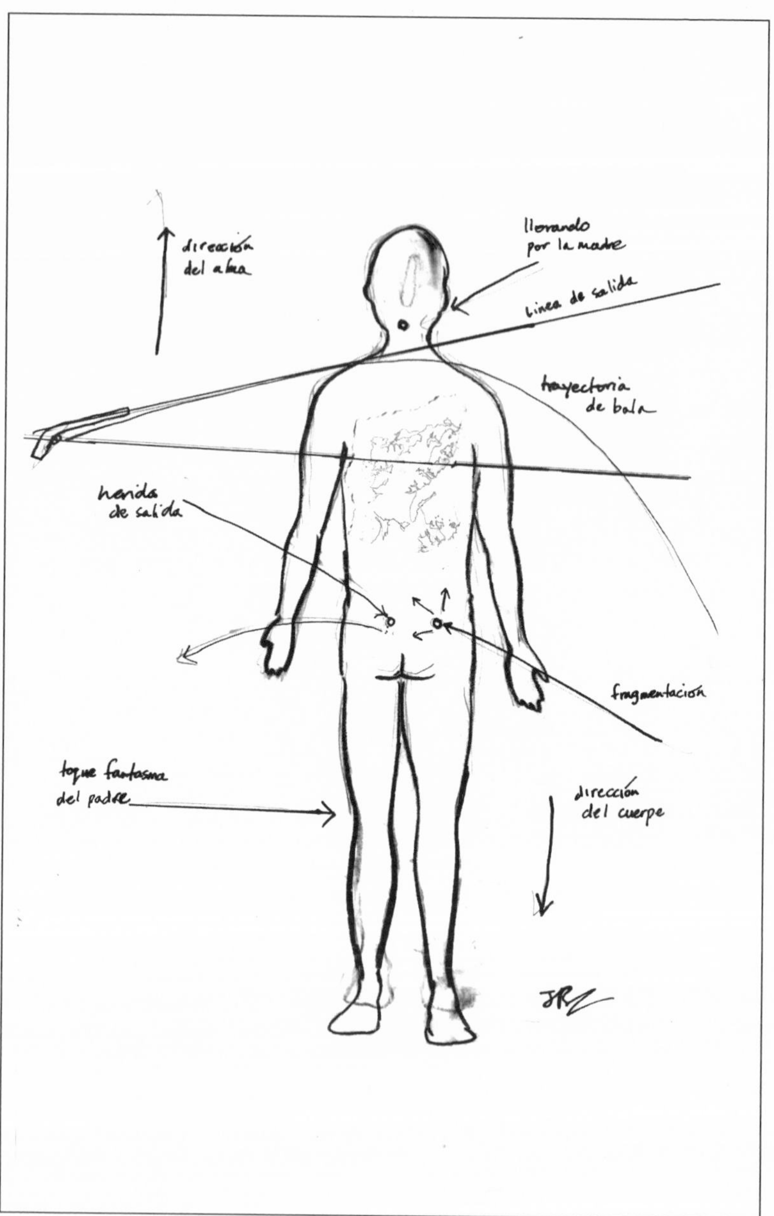

FIGURE 2: *José Ramírez, 1989.* Fragmentación *(preliminary sketch); pen and ink, collage, chalk.*

FIGURE 3: *José Ramírez, 1991.* Mujer Oso *(preliminary sketch); pen and ink.*

FIGURE 4: *José Ramírez, 1993.* Saltamontes y Cucarachas *(cartoon); pen and ink.*

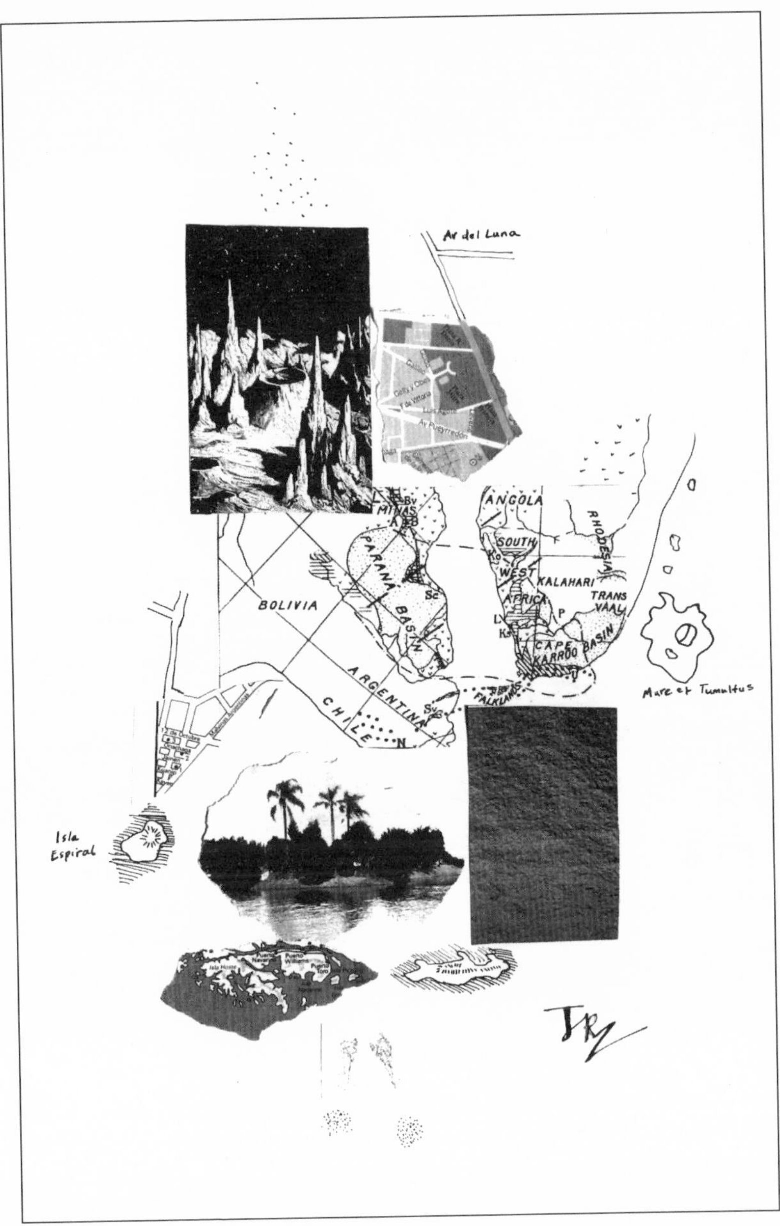

FIGURE 5: *José Ramírez, 1996.* Avenida de la Luna; *collage, pen and ink.*

FIGURE 6: *José Ramírez, 1984. Sketchbook page:* Fotografía; *chalk, pencil.*

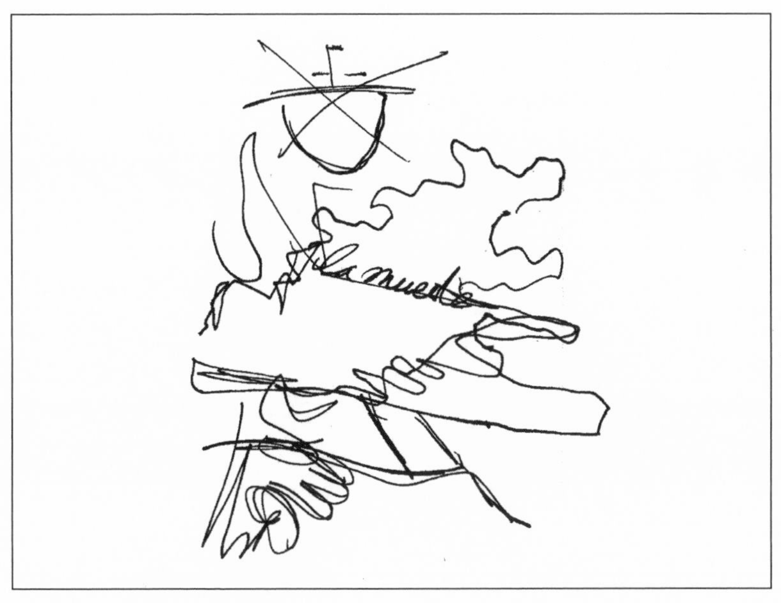

FIGURE 7: *Miguel's note.*

FIGURE 8: *John Gerrard Keulemans, 1890.* Antarctic wolf.

FIGURE 9: *José Ramírez, 1980. Sketchbook page:* La tumba de Rufina Cambacérès; *chalk, pencil.*

PART TWO

I

"Alice is not my real name."

This is her confession, the woman he has tied up on the bed. He is not surprised. Of course she is not who she claimed to be. Neither is he. He came to Spain over a year ago. Every day he bludgeons his sibilance and refines his accent, attempting to fit in.

"What is it, then?"

"Guess."

The woman whose name is not Alice is anchored to his bedstead with four chiffon scarves. Looking at her naked body, he sees his opposite. Her back is freckled, muscular and warm. Her legs open to a stranger. She is alive. He is a ghost.

He begins to lick her feet. They taste of the sea. He will work his way up. This prize of his, this piece of English flesh, so close he could crush and destroy it. He encircles one of her ankles with his fingers. His numb hand looks strong. What will he do if she notices the long white scars around his wrists? He lets go and walks to the window.

He knows almost nothing about this woman whose name is not Alice, yet he senses that she too has fortified herself. He has seen it in her eyes. He has sensed the tiniest flinch, the secret slide of an iron portcullis behind her smile as his face moves toward hers.

The window reflects furled white sheets.

"Do you like the cold?" he asks.

She turns her head but makes no attempt to free herself. The gauze curtain sways.

He needs air.

*

He met her in the Barcelona fruit market where she was holding half a dragon fruit, examining its speckled insides. He watched her until she looked up and met his gaze. Blue eyes. A polite smile. He smiled back and raised his eyebrows. She looked back at the dragon fruit, a headless pink reptile with green flippers. For a moment, he was almost entirely certain they had met before. Then she turned away and her hair fell, veiling her hands. Nevertheless, he sensed she was waiting for him.

She looked up again over the mounds of cherries to where he was standing, feeling foolish with his half-eaten peach.

"Excuse me, but do I know you?"

After six months in London, his English was much improved. Since moving to Barcelona he had met a few English tourists, but most of his friends were also from South America: numerous Argentinian exiles, a couple on the run from Chile, an Uruguayan singer, the Colombian janitor of his apartment building; no Catalans, although he has tried learning the language. The Spanish he speaks with his friends has become a hybrid, a rootless mix of dialects that varies depending on whom he is with. English is the language in which he works but does not live. Still, he prides himself on spotting Brits of whatever descent: Indian, Jamaican, Caucasian. He likes watching them make their way through the city, fumbling and giggling, defensive and arrogant. On weekend afternoons during the first month he was here, he would follow them around, track their progress through all the tourist spots and sketch what he saw. Elderly women in saris, mouths covered by scarves as if to hide their disdain; fat, white teenage girls with sunburned cleavage bending down to coo at caged finches; middle-aged men in too-tight socks tripping over street dogs.

"I don't think so." The woman replaced the fruit and wiped her hands on her shirt.

"Oh. I'm sorry. I thought I saw you at Antonio's party." He was lying, of course.

"Antonio?"

"Antonio from Uruguay."

"No. No." The woman smiled. "You have mistaken me for someone else." Her voice was languid, yet there was a wariness in her eyes. He felt seen.

"Well. Would you like a coffee then?"

But she was already leaving, walking briskly through the market, her painted toes delicately stepping over spilt crushed ice. He followed. The woman's red hair hung down her back. He wanted to touch it. Perhaps he could persuade her to meet him for dinner.

"I am not an asshole," he yelled out after her. A phrase he had learned from television.

Ten yards ahead, she turned and spoke imperiously over her shoulder. "And you aren't *Spanish,* either. You're something else." Her eyes were sharp, glittering with amusement. She was not young—small wrinkles were visible around her eyes. He jogged up to meet her. Her knuckles whitened as she gripped her handbag.

He pressed on. "And you do not wear the rucksack. Nor the…"

He indicated his waistline with his hands. What was the word for those ugly belts?

"Fanny pack. God, no." Now she was laughing. She had stopped walking and they stood facing each other, allowing the crowds to shuffle past on either side. He straightened his shirt. She was not a tourist exactly, and yet she had to be visiting, her freckled arms leanly guarding her body while she examined him at close range.

"I was wondering..."

"Let's have coffee. I have a few minutes." She looked back at him, delighted by the surprise on his face.

"Where are you from?"

"Montevideo." He grinned, feeling puppyish. The lie came easily enough. He thrust his hands into his pockets. "I work here in Barcelona, but you know I lived in your country for quite a while. You are from London?"

They were walking now, a truce declared, acquaintances heading politely down the Avenida, away from the market and back toward Las Ramblas, where the human statues were already out in force.

"No, I'm from the north, near Manchester. But for the past two years I've been living in Greece."

"Greece?" This was unexpected, although perhaps it explained her apparent ease. Greece was a country he had never visited. Instantly he found himself wanting to go there, if only to understand more of this woman he was following. The hem of her turquoise dress brushed momentarily against him.

"Yes, Greece." She held out her hand. "Alice Barrow."

He took it. Warm, sinewy, angled with sharp rings. He wondered what kind of business deal he was sealing. "José Ramírez."

The sun was already fierce. He felt excited, light-headed.

In his pockets were his keys and his empty wallet. He had no cash to pay for coffee. There were stacks of empty bottles in his apartment, which stank of burnt toast and dirty laundry. His hair was thinning. His boss was disgusted by his inability to meet deadlines, although he grudgingly admitted his work was good. Very good.

Alice led the way past the Liceu and the department stores, to the older part of Las Ramblas, and stopped in front of Cafè de l'Òpera. It was, as usual, filled with men and the odd tourist sipping an espresso. He did not usually come here, but Alice seemed to want to. No doubt it was on her list of top ten places to visit. He sat down mutely, feeling a little nauseated as he patted his empty pockets. Hopefully Alice Barrow had not spent all her change in the market.

"I must be insane," she said, leaning forward over the polished tabletop. "Going out for coffee with a stranger from Uruguay." She ran her left hand through her hair. "Perhaps you do this sort of thing all the time."

He changed the subject. "What did you dream of last night?"

"Dream of? I don't remember. I never remember my dreams unless I'm really ill, and then they're dreadful." Her finger drew shapes on the tabletop as they waited for their coffees. Then she wiped them away.

"I dreamt I was in the market and saw a woman who reminded me of someone."

She looked up sharply.

Their coffees arrived. The lip of his cup was slightly chipped. He took a sip. Alice Barrow smiled.

He had just ended an awkward affair with a Chilean, a beautiful but ferocious young woman named Elena, whose artistic ambitions resulted in his spending large amounts of time tied up in bondage while she drew him, meticulously, in graphite and charcoal. He had to hide inside himself to do it, had to smoke a lot of hashish and drink a lot of whisky, because bondage brought him back to that hillside. Elena knew none of this, although she may have guessed it. She was a torture survivor herself. Rape, judging by the way she disassociated whenever they had sex lying down.

They mostly fucked standing up. After, he would submit to the bondage and she would draw him and he would relive his past. She would draw while wearing only her underpants, one leg lifted, hip out to the side, and he would study her feet. They were the loveliest part of her: arched, slender, soft. She posed for him a few times. It made him feel young again, drawing innocently, his artistic intent not perverted by the need to make money, no need to shake off the ghost of his father, whose voice was always there, in the background, reciting Homer.

"I think I recognize you, too," said Alice. *Code word nautilus.*

He put down his cup. "What do you mean?"

"I don't know," she said, now drawing circles in a circle of spilt coffee. He pulled a clean handkerchief out of his sleeve and offered it to her. It was one of the handkerchiefs his mother had made for him when he started high school, with his initials, *JR*, embroidered in white thread across one corner.

Rosa had met a new man who encouraged her to stop working. Perhaps she would even move in with him, to Recoleta, a house without dust, and with no reminders of her past. She told José he would be welcome any time, as long as he did not walk around in his underwear or leave his artwork lying about.

"My mother made this for me. I miss her."

"Do you?" She looked at him with curiosity.

"Alice Barrow," he said, stroking her thin wrist. His hands felt tender: needy little animals. "I am not a very good man."

Alice gently pulled her hand away but left it on the tabletop.

"I wouldn't know. But you do remind me of someone I know."

"Oh?"

"You are very much like him. You are mirror images."

❦

His soul has gone rogue since Ushuaia, walking by itself into walls, if not right through them, taking his consciousness hostage and running with it into the night, into the ground. Some days he wakes and doesn't know where it has been, smells, sounds, voices erupting. At these times, he does not know where he is from, or where he lives, his life rewinding and repeating like a spliced documentary.

Ever since Ushuaia he has been drawing wounds.

There is still a hole in him, the shape of his father. He has not heard Carlos's voice for over twenty years. José's rational mind believes him to be dead, thrown out of some helicopter and dumped over the Atlantic Ocean following apprehension and torture in a place known as the Athletic Club. But there are times when José doubts this.

Increasingly, his mind insists there is a version of Carlos living safely in Ireland, in the body of another man: Ulises Pereira. José has wondered if, in his grief, he invented him. But he has not: Pereira simply appeared one day, intact. The anti-Carlos. Sr. Ulises Pereira, who teaches Latin American Studies at University College Dublin and translates contemporary Irish fiction and poetry into Spanish. He has a limp and walks, audibly, with a cane. His hair is grey and he wears wire-framed glasses, quite different from those Carlos left behind. The scars on this old man's body are closed mouths. They speak inwards, into bone and sinew.

Carlos Ramírez is dead. Ulises has left Dublin in search of

José, walking the streets in a long grey overcoat like an American spy. He does not sleep. Who can sleep when everything in the northern hemisphere, including justice, hangs upside down? The stars are wrong, the months, the years and the seasons. Those who deserve nothing have it all. If he wishes to live on, Ulises Pereira must cannibalize Carlos Ramírez, the poor bastard who did not outlive his dreams.

José first saw Ulises emerging from a neighbouring office building. Ulises stopped and returned his stare. His face was Carlos's, but slightly fleshier, weary and lined, with pouches under the eyes. "Excuse me," said José, but a passerby clipped him on the shoulder, and when he looked up, Ulises had turned away.

He glanced up and down the sidewalk. He wondered who could see them, this heavier, older version of his father staring impassively at a crazed, younger version of himself. He tried to distract himself with the pretty girls, their heels clicking as they passed by on their way to the Calle Florida. But he couldn't help staring at the old man. His clothes were old-fashioned, not at all like Carlos's. A green velvet waistcoat, glasses on a chain.

José turned to leave. Soon the man fell into step beside him.

"You do not exist. You are a ghost," he said aloud.

Silence. José turned back to the man, who smiled, revealing tobacco-stained teeth.

José examined the spider cracks in the lenses of the old man's glasses. "You have been following me ever since Ushuaia."

Ulises placed his hand on José's arm. The touch felt real.

José's eyes burned. *You are not my father. You are only a ghost.*

"My dear boy," whispered Pereira, leaning over and kissing José on both cheeks.

José touched his face. Saliva.

Then Pereira was gone.

She dives beneath the surface. The lake is cold, mercifully stripping all feeling as she plunges quickly into its depths. She's a good swimmer. Not afraid of travelling far from shore. Her parents aren't watching, and probably didn't even hear the splash. They're up on the bank, setting out a nice little picnic: boiled eggs, roast ham, pickled onions. The flask of tea and Kendal Mint Cake. It's the last week of May, and the weather is finally clement. The trees are bright with new leaves, and in the field beside the caravan site are dozens of long-limbed lambs.

No one would think the country was at war. Jane herself finds it difficult to believe. She travelled here by train with a half-empty rucksack, irritated to be pulled from her shared student house, where large tubs of tahini are stashed in the kitchen, courtesy of the food co-op. Where a giant Maggie Thatcher dart board, pitted with holes, hangs above the toilet. She'd been too busy studying to think or feel. But then her parents called and invited her to join them.

"We'll be selling the caravan soon," said her mother. "One last summer." There was a slight pause. "Dad's bringing his transistor radio, so we can all keep abreast of the news."

Down here, no one can see her. She luxuriates in private, holds her breath for as long as she can, opening her eyes to peer into the dark, where she knows, somewhere, an entire village lies hidden, drowned sixty years ago when the valley was flooded. As a small child, she wasn't allowed to swim here. *Too cold; too deep.* Instead she spent ages staring into the depths in the hopes of seeing a chimney stack or a church spire. Wouldn't it be a dreamy place to live—empty of people, quiet, and full of fish? She imagined swimming between houses, visiting each in turn, gliding over rooftops.

For a moment she sees streetlight.

She surfaces, gasping. Blows her nose, shakes the water from her hair. There is no streetlight.

Her body is on fire, ignited by the terrible cold of the water.

She swims for shore, hauls out on the stony beach, and towels off vigorously before dropping her sweatshirt over her head and retrieving her flip-flops. Twenty minutes have passed and she hasn't once thought of her brother, of cameras, hand grenades, or casualties.

I shall *kill a man. Men, if I must.* Peter's last, half-goading words to his pacifist sister, before he left for the South Atlantic.

"Are you coming, love?" calls her mother, from above the bracken. "Dad's chilly, and it looks like it's going to rain."

José had a dream the night he arrived in Barcelona, exhausted after the train journey from London. That night he stayed in a cheap hotel, his only lead a name on a business card, a man named Ricardo he had met in a West End pub who had claimed there was work to be had on the Continent, illustrating medical textbooks for students. It was November: a filthy month in Britain, rain darkening the sky so it seemed like night even during the lunch hour. Barcelona sparkled. He had to shield his eyes as he stood at the entrance to Gaudí's cathedral. José had read how the architect had been run over by a tram.

Look, he is here, whispered Pereira. José looked up and there sat the old man on a marble bench, smoking. *He's dreaming you.* José allowed the hopefulness to drown him, just for a moment, before anyone else came by, before dragging his heavy feet back to the little pension filled with silverfish and long-legged spiders, where he lay down and dreamed of a wolf. Dreams within dreams.

When he woke, he remembered the woman standing in the cathedral. He got out his sketchbook and pencils and hastily drew her, her face lifted, gazing up to a place which could have been heaven. He drew her hair, pulled back into a bun, the small, thin scar on the temple he'd noticed before turning to leave. He had been overwhelmed by her beauty and the evidence of an injury that was clearly deliberate, for what other than a knife would make such a clean line? Who was she?

José watched Alice drawing her circles on the dark mahogany table. He reached across and swept back her hair, pulling it to the right to examine her skin but there was nothing. No sharp red line or bump of keloid joining the top of her left ear with her scalp. He let the hair go.

"I have been looking for you," she said. "But instead you found me."

❦

The evening after he had seen Pereira for the first time, he noticed a sheaf of papers had been stuffed into his case. Drawings, notes—it all looked very confusing until he reached the last page: a copy of the warrah drawing he once found in the back of a book, and beneath it, a pencilled-in question mark.

It was getting dark. He broke into a run along the avenue, passing men and women entering cafés. The sound of laughter chased him to the subway.

At home, and by lamplight, he examined the scribbled-over papers, unfolding a stiff, slightly musty piece of foolscap. An academic treatise, typed in English. Was it his own? He placed his old green suitcase on the bed. Its straps reminded him of his mother's old bathing costume, a pleated, pale green affair complete with corset. She wore it with a rubber bathing cap decorated with flowers, a child's cap. She had a small head. One day, when he was about eight, he found the bathing costume crumpled up at the back of his mother's wardrobe. It smelled of rubber; slightly illicit. He stepped inside the wardrobe and tried it on.

⸙

He pulled out his sketch of the woman at the cathedral and found Alice looked nothing like her. Alice was lean yet broad, her bones visible under the muscles that slid like slow water, back and forth. The woman in the sketch was soft-bodied, loose and diaphanous, her hair a cloud of angry spirals, but tied back, unlike Alice's cool bronze. He closed the book. It gave up dust. He opened it again and examined the scar he had drawn, a line of crimson pencil marking her temple, like the template for an incision. He had seen such marks on the bodies of corpses. He closed the book. He did not want to look at the sketch.

She was not Alice.

He had been commissioned to draw a series of medical brochures, to illustrate the effects of smoking, to demonstrate the early stages of pregnancy, the ideal placement of intrauterine devices. The brochures would be written in Spanish and Catalan and distributed all over the city, patients from every quarter privy to his masterpieces as they sat in the waiting rooms of their local surgeries and contemplated the consequences of their actions. It wasn't the kind of artistic fame he'd once contemplated, but at least it was better than working in a third-rate design office or cutting up sandwiches for pinstripe-suited office workers the way he had in London. Later, handing out nightclub flyers outside tube stations while holding down a job in a Mexican restaurant, barely able to stand up for exhaustion. What was the point? To keep moving. To avoid getting stuck. If he stands still too long the cold returns. Aching in his bones, nerve pain in his feet and hands, headaches that leave him thumping his fist into the wall.

It took him a month in London to find work as an illustrator. It was easy enough to lie about his qualifications and his portfolio spoke for itself. He had found a girlfriend. Her name was Claire. She reminded him of Gaby. Claire was a waitress who was really an actress, who was really an artist, quick to laugh, but with a desperate intensity to her gaze. Claire, it turned out, wanted to get married. She wanted to have kids. They agreed he would marry her and apply for citizenship. After three bottles of wine, it all looked so simple. Together they would live in one of the suburbs and commute into the city like civilized people.

He talked himself into it. Marriage would be good for him. What better way to silence the anti-Carlos, to seal over the open grave of his past?

He moved into a flat with Claire and her friends, and for three months they collaborated in a tragic theatrical performance together, the courtship of fools. He ended up staying in London for more than a year, even after their relationship collapsed. He had thought of going home but could not face it. Buenos Aires was a mystery to him. All he would meet if he returned would be his own reflection, glinting off the black marble wall monument, with its lists of the Malvinas dead. No medals would be awarded him. Dishonour burns.

His jilting of Claire scorched a ring of earth around his heart. He had known the whole thing was wrong after three days, his hands delicately stroking her thinnest skin, fingers slipping faster and faster as she opened further, the way his thoughts closed down as he was drawn down into the lie.

The whole time he was in London, he made an effort to never, ever discuss the war he had fought against these people, the Battle of Mount Longdon, the hand grenades and the messages from Menéndez: *TO ARMS! TO BATTLE!* If he admitted to being Argentine, he was bombarded with questions. When did you leave? Did you fight in the war? What made you want to come here? Over and over he had endured the stares, and over and over he had repeated his invented narrative, that he did not fight, he had been too young, remembered it only vaguely. He listened to the British attacking their own government loudly, animatedly and publicly, as if there could be no penalty.

Dipping his nib into ink, José detailed the alveoli of a young man in the pink of health, despite being sliced vertically in two. Then came the pleural membrane. As usual, his lines were perfectly controlled. He had long since lost the tremor he used to have holding a pen. Not that his remaining fingers had fully healed. But he had grown so adept at accommodating their limits that his drawing was better than ever. The hours he spent at his light table were his best. Sometimes he let his mind wander, let it slide across the surfaces of memories like a cloth polishing glass. At those times, nothing hurt him. Even the image of his father, head bowed into a book, would not cause him to tremble. During those times he dreamed, steering a ship across a windless lake. Images appeared, moving and speaking as he sailed silently by. He was both alive and yet dead, a perfectly pressed flower.

Alice Barrow. After their cups were drained, the pastry crumbs on the white plates drying in the heat, she had paid for it all, and left abruptly. Yet he had stroked her hand, and she had not withdrawn it.

Who was she looking for?

José uncapped his red ink. Why had he told her his birthplace was Montevideo? Perhaps he should return. Sometimes it feels like Miguel has never left him. The two of them drinking sherry with the Chileans, swapping stories of lost virginities and dictatorship. Sometimes he can turn to his left and for a moment wonder why Miguel has not yet returned from the bathroom.

His apartment was cool. It was also quiet: siesta time. He rarely napped. He liked to work through the dog hours, even welcomed the sleepiness, which allowed daydreams. By four in the afternoon he would be done and would phone the office, report on his progress, and listen to his boss for as much time as decorum dictated, then hang up. The evening was for walking, for smoking on street corners and visiting bars. Not such a bad life: the Argentine Abroad.

She knows who you are, whispered Pereira.

His hand faltered, smudging the curve of the diaphragm. The old man's hand appeared and hovered for a moment above his.

Then came a knock on the door.

"Yes?" He stepped away from his desk, away from the man.

It was Alice.

She glanced past him into the hallway after sliding off her oversized sunglasses. "I waited until you were a block ahead and then I followed you home. But I had forgotten your name, so I couldn't work out which apartment you lived in. I had to ask a young woman in camouflage trousers."

"I see. What do you want?" José curled his toes under and then straightened them.

"I wanted to see where you live."

For a moment, José considered closing the door, then stepped aside. She put down her bag. She was wearing red lipstick, dark blue leather sandals that revealed her toes, painted an odd shade of orange.

"You live alone?"

"Yes."

"I am staying in the Nouvel Catalunya."

"Are you going back to Athens?"

"No. I'm finished there."

"I see." José walked to his light table and turned off the light. He carefully placed a piece of vellum over his drawing, and then for good measure, a heavy book on top of that. "Would you like coffee?"

"No, thanks. Maybe some water."

José went into his tiny kitchen and poured her a glass of Barcelona tap water.

"So, what is this? Are you stalking me?"

Alice laughed but did not answer. Then her look turned serious. She took a long gulp of water.

"I approached you," he said, "because I thought I recognized you. You remind me of a woman I saw in a dream on my first night here. But this woman had a scar on her forehead." He indicated the line from temple to hair in a swift, brutal motion with his left index finger. "And you do not." He paused. "I can show you the sketches."

Alice looked as if she were about to reveal something, but said only, "I wish I could draw."

"Everyone can draw. It's simply a question of how much time you put into it. If you drew every day you would quickly improve. Here. Start." He flung a sketchpad at her.

"Okay." She sat down cross-legged on the rug. He could see her underwear. She opened the sketchpad and picked up the pencil he passed to her.

"Don't think. Just make lines. Let the pencil tell you what it wants to make."

"All right." Alice closed her eyes. She pressed the pencil hard into the page, so hard it broke the lead. She opened her eyes and examined it. "There. I made a dot."

"Excellent," said José. "Welcome to the world of Joan Miró."

"You are making fun of me." Alice picked up the pencil again and unpeeled the wood until a small stub of lead was exposed. "Here: you draw."

"This is not much of a tool." He licked the lead. "Nevertheless, I will try." He glanced up at her. He sketched a horse, its head stretched out, legs tumbling in a blurry gallop. "There."

"Is it me?"

"No. You can see it is a horse."

"Bravo." Alice ripped the picture out of the sketchpad and placed it beside her on the rug.

"Now you have original artwork from a genuine Barcelona artist to put up on your wall in Athens or London."

"My brother used to draw, but he stopped. Too bad, really. He was a good artist. I never did, at least not much. He was always so much better. I hated what I did."

"You must have been good at something."

"Yes, school. Writing essays. Keeping my mouth shut and ignoring other people."

"But now you are loud."

"Really? Do you think so?" She snorted. "Not anymore. I'm quite boring. A mediocre expat."

He kissed her. Slowly at first, experimentally, as if exploring a new wine. Then she kissed him back. They lay down on the rug, its pattern a series of concentric ovals, each darker than the last.

She took off her dress, slipping it over her head, her hair lifting wildly for a moment. He smoothed it, enjoying the quick stab of electricity. Then he touched her breasts, large and pale. He took one in his mouth, caressing the nipple with his tongue.

Traitor, whispered Pereira.

How long had it been since he touched English skin? The flush of pink over blue veins in her neck translucent as soft chalk layered over grey paper. He took off his shirt.

❧

He looked at his captive. She was naked, her hair loose around her face. "You are beautiful," he said. He lay down next to her, and gently, with great care, began to make love to her. They continued until the light was almost gone and the colours of their bodies became only form. He rolled on his back. The curtain billowed. Out beyond the iron railings of the balcony a moped raced and voices lifted, the fever of evening settling on the narrow back street where sometimes a band would spill out from the crowded, hot bar and play until two in the morning.

"Would you like a drink?" His voice sounded thick and strange. What he wanted was a cigarette.

"Yes."

"Let's go to the bar. It's just over the road. Or we can go somewhere else."

He sat up and began putting on his clothes.

Alice did not move. "Do we have to go anywhere?" The space between them suddenly loomed.

"No," he said, turning to face her. "But I need some air." She looked at him. There was something in the room between them.

"I should go."

"I can walk you to your hotel."

Alice sat up and pulled one of the discarded sheets around her body. "Is something wrong?"

Careful, whispered Pereira. *You are in the hands of the enemy.*

He felt around in his dresser drawer for the pack of cigarettes he knew he had left there. He struck a cardboard match and the whole room glowed.

Later, they sat at the bar downstairs, drinking Malbec. It seemed as good a time as any to tell her the truth. "I am not from Uruguay, I am Argentine."

The inevitable question. "Did you fight in the war?"

"I don't like to talk about it, especially to you Brits. Too much—schadenfreude."

"Aha." Alice fidgeted with her napkin. He glanced about, wondered whether they would bump into anyone he knew. Usually he avoided this place. But the noise made it easier to be together.

"This is my ex," said Alice. She placed a photograph of a dark-haired man in a white shirt standing on a beach on the table between them.

"Good looking."

"I suppose. But it didn't work out."

"And so, you come to Barcelona, on your way back home."

"I don't have a home."

"None of us do." He drained the last of his Malbec.

Then he saw the other photo on the table: two men in red berets, British Paras. Alice pushed the photograph toward José, who did not pick it up. His stomach clenched.

"Is this your purpose? You come here to show me this?"

Alice reached for the snapshot. José got there first, lifted it up and turned it over: *Aldershot, 1982.* An ice shard pierced the back of his neck. He said nothing. In the low light of the bar, her face was arresting in its intensity. He thought of a painting, a dark Dutch interior, ripe fruit balanced on pewter plates, Alice with her hair inside a white linen cap, leaning out of, or perhaps into, a doorway.

"That man is my brother. He..."

José interrupted. "Horse."

"What?"

"Don't forget your horse. I believe it is sitting on my coffee table." What mattered right now was to get her out of here; not to let her know how he felt.

"No, I have it here." She took out the sketch.

"Like Mary Poppins, huh, this bag of yours? Soon you will take out a lamp and perhaps a measuring tape."

Alice put money on the table and stood, prepared to leave. He stood also, held out her coat.

"May I walk you to your hotel?" *Watch out,* whispered Pereira. *This is how they trap you.*

"Listen. You can say no if you like but would you like to go somewhere tomorrow, take the day off? I'm leaving on Sunday." Alice was speaking too quickly, avoiding looking at him.

"All right." It was ridiculous. Positively dangerous. His heart beat too fast, his throat felt dry. Besides which, he had not even finished the first basic outline and the entire set of drafts was due by Monday. "Meet me at the Café at eleven. And bring your camera." If she was not finished with him, then he was not finished with her, either. He would give her something to photograph.

11

Ten months ago, fresh from Buenos Aires, José had stood at the bottom of a relentless escalator and tried to manoeuvre his suitcase onto the steps.

"Excuse me." A woman in a red-striped dress and stilettos picked her way past. The young white men in shirtsleeves barged by. José heaved his bag onto the next step and watched as it tumbled down again. When he eventually made it to the top, scudding clouds greeted him: the English month of May. Damaged by rough handling on the plane, the suitcase had burst open like a jacaranda onto the street, spilling unwashed laundry and sketchbook pages across the pollen-painted pavement. A wind rose, and a pair of his boxer shorts wrapped themselves around the trunk of a tree. Fuck you, thought José, watching his faded red t-shirt fill with air. He took what remained of his belongings and crammed them into the case, carried it up the steps of a cheap hotel.

Brochures for Madame Tussauds and boat tours on the Thames sat neatly piled in racks just inside the glass door that swished over a triangle of red carpet. It smelled of fried eggs and cabbage, cleaning fluid and furniture polish. After checking in and surrendering his luggage to a porter, he stepped quickly up the dimly lit stairs and down the corridor to where his suitcase waited, tied up temporarily with rope.

"Your room, sir." The key seemed ridiculously long. It opened a door into a shabby high-ceilinged room. Water pipes snaked by, leading to a rust-stained sink. The tap dripped. An iron bedstead stretched out from the wall. Traffic hissed on the street—a sash window, stuck partly open: it could neither open nor close any further.

José began to cry. He sat on the bed and waited for the tears to pass. Then he undressed, washed in the sink, and put on a clean short-sleeved shirt before heading out again. The ancient woman at the desk cocked her head at him, her eyes bright.

"Finding everything all right there, love?"

He nodded then pushed out clumsily into the street.

He could call Gaby long-distance. Her number was written on the back of the paper on which he had scrawled *National Portrait Gallery*. There was a photograph of James Joyce which Carlos wrote about. He was pretty sure the photograph was at this gallery. He recalled that the gallery was on the main square, or close to it anyway, and he felt a sense of urgency. On the Tube he studied the complicated little map: did Carlos ever make it here? He went on a trip to Europe when he was younger, before he met Rosa, and had visited Greece as well. José drew his finger over the map's coloured lines.

"Know where you're going, sir?" A man in uniform approached him, smelling of tobacco.

"Yes, thank you." It wasn't quite true, but José smiled. On the platform he pushed through the barrier like a drowning man. The human river dragged him with it, away from the platform and up into a sudden spring chill. Small white blossoms dotted the trees. London stank of hot metal and burning soot. At the National Portrait Gallery he asked the docent in halting English about "a photograph... not a painting, but a photograph of the author of the book *Ulysses*?" He clutched his leather briefcase close to his body, hoped it did not appear suspicious. He did not want to set it down for a moment. He knew there were fears about terrorists.

The docent did not seem to notice. Instead her eyes lit up. "Yes, yes!" She leaned in, her teeth the uneven focal point of her cubist face. "You mean the Freund, dear. Not English. German. Most active in the 1930s..." Her lecture continued as she walked him with clicking heels through various serene white rooms until they found it, hung in a side gallery, the walls painted red, the lights low.

"Thank you. *Gracias.*" José made an absurd bow.

"Not at all." The docent nodded, her eyes lidded again, the scroll of her knowledge rolled up with a flick of a uniformed wrist.

He read the caption: *Freund photographed Joyce on three occasions; this session, in his apartment in the Rue Edmund Valentin in Paris, was for a* Time *magazine cover and was taken in the year in which his most revolutionary novel,* Finnegan's Wake, *was published.*

What did Gisèle Freund look like? José's school art teacher once remarked that all portraits resemble their painters. He wondered if the same were true for photographers. In the photograph, James Joyce held something shiny up against his chin. He appeared wistful, his elongated chin a buffer against border guards, tax collectors and diapers. Perhaps he wished he had not written such big books, tomes that took decades to read, let alone translate.

Now just relax, Herr Joyce. José imagined the German woman with the camera. He imagined Rosa, less patient, circling her husband with her Kodak on the Mar del Plata, her orange two-piece bathing suit framing her taut belly. *Look at the ocean! Smile!* In the picture Carlos was blurry, bleached out. He never did vacations well. Rosa despaired of ever getting a decent picture of them together.

Freund's James Joyce had an asymmetric face, split into irreconcilable halves, his circular glasses framing eyes that disagreed, one looking down and to the right in an expression of regret, the other hugely magnified and turned skyward. In his hands, tucked beneath his chin, the writer held a third lens filled with abstract striations of darkness and light. The chair Joyce sat in was the colour of old, dried blood.

"Longest way round is the shortest way home."—JJ. Meet me here, beneath this picture and I will tell you a joke—but first…

First what? This incomplete sentence was written in black ballpoint pen on the back of a postcard Rosa discovered when she finally went through Carlos's papers. The card was tucked into the typescript of a talk he was scheduled to deliver at the James Joyce Society's annual symposium in Barcelona in 1977: *The Secret War of the Unconscious Mind.* She had given it to José after it turned up, hidden behind a cabinet in Carlos's office at the university. Someone had been emptying rooms before they took the building down.

"Did he mean to escape?" José asked his mother.

"He considered exile."

Joyce peered out of the photograph into the future, worried, sad, exhausted from intellectual labour, his failure to change a world that was drifting toward war.

The last photograph taken of Carlos depicted him in his office, that little room just off the living room where he spent most of his time when he wasn't out. The photo was taken by Rosa in a fit of frustration—once again he was not coming to dinner. José remembered his mother asking Carlos to smile, and as his father turned around in his chair and looked up, astonished, the shutter clicked.

José glanced round to make sure no one was watching,

looked down at the unfinished postcard and tucked it inside the picture frame, along with a folded-up response.

"So I came, Papi. And now…"

"Can I help you?" It was the docent again. The note fell to the floor. *Code word: 'nautilus,' Papi, if you are still alive…*

"Please don't litter," she commanded, but José was already halfway down the corridor, the faces of British Modernists flickering by.

Outside, he lit up a cigarette and inhaled. A young man rolled restlessly around on a bench, a bottle dangling from his hand. In the Houses of Parliament, it was no longer Mrs. Thatcher but a weak-chinned minor character by the name of Major who was sending young men off to war. He remembered that later, full-colour photograph of Thatcher in a headscarf and goggles, seated in the cab of a tank, somewhere in Germany. A portrait of a victor, her smile of tombstones; a bust of a woman, hollow.

He would sign up for English lessons. He would study illustration. In this way, he would turn back time, roll back over his past selves like a reversing Challenger tank and become a victor himself, not a pathetic beast. He found a public telephone outside the museum and dialed a number, pumped in a ridiculous amount of change.

"Hello? Is Gabriella there?"

A man answered. Gruff. "Who's calling?"

"A friend. She gave me this number."

"Well, Gaby is out. Can I take a message?"

José rested his head against the cold metal. After a pause, he recited the number of his hotel. But it was too late by then. He had already run out of time.

The next day, José approached the Imperial War Museum's imposing entrance through its Italian-style garden, where cannons were displayed between green lawns, among budding rose bushes.

"I'll tell you something…" Over breakfast that morning, the elderly waitress pointed at the colour brochure he was reading. "That building there used to be a loony bin!"

"You mean a mental hospital?" José struggled to translate.

"Yes, dear." The waitress flourished her notepad, clicked on her ballpoint. "Used to lock 'em up and throw away the key. Now, white or brown?"

"Brown."

"Tea or coffee?"

"Coffee."

"Bedlam. Short for Bethlehem. Used to be run like a zoo. Scrambled or fried?"

Climbing the steps José noticed his full stomach. A man in a navy blue blazer approached him slowly. "Here for the special exhibition, sir?"

"No, thanks. I would like to visit the front lines."

The man, whose moustache was waxed at both tips, waved him through. His shoes squeaked across the parquet. Not many visitors. He entered a twilit gallery, glass vitrines on all sides filled with World War II memorabilia. He examined a child's red gas mask, its louvred snout and circular eyes putting him in mind of a butchered pig. Next to it was a small stuffed dog, grey and worn, which, according to the caption, was given as a good luck token to Private Edward Scholes by his younger sister Pamela before he set off for Malaysia, and later Borneo, in 1942. Scholes returned alive, it explained, but only after incarceration in a prisoner of war camp where he was miraculously able to hide the stuffed dog and later return with it, as the interpretive sign read, "a little the worse for wear."

José wanted to steal the dog.

Two rooms away was a model of a World War I trench, complete with dead Tommies littering its mud floor, just the kind of *son et lumière* show to trigger flashbacks. He paused, his throat tightening as if in a noose. He loosened his belt a notch. Then he fell forward, tripped over a ladder, and fell to the bottom of the trench. There was a high-pitched squeal, and then a boom, and he was clutching his head, curled at the base of the exhibit in fetal position.

If he died of a heart attack here, no one would know.

He raised his head. The shooting had stopped and the only other presence in the gallery was a mannequin dressed in a WWI British infantry uniform, its bucket-like helmet striated by explosions of light. Grenades exploded in José's skull. His neck vibrated with the judder of small arms fire, a black sky beneath his feet. He tried to orient himself, to listen for the voice of his lieutenant, but there was no one, only the cold stripping the skin off his hands and face.

He pulled himself to his feet. He staggered a little. It was hot and also cold. He should get out now. Instead he headed back to the entrance, asked the guard if there was an exhibit about the Malvinas War.

"Do you mean the Falklands conflict? There is no such gallery." The guard's face was the colour of a ripe plum. "However, there is a display wall located in the Contemporary Conflicts Room." He indicated a yellow arrow on the floor.

Briefcase clutched to chest, José followed the arrow and almost bumped into a middle-aged man who was standing at the far end of the gallery reading a Spanish-language guidebook.

José looked up, wiped his mouth. Ulises Pereira. *Mierda.* He had hoped to outrun him, but now they were face to face.

⸙

Pereira invited José to join him in the museum café, with its astonishing array of English cakes, each granted its own glass pedestal and sliced provocatively to reveal a kind of dainty crotch. After some deliberation, José selected a plain yellow cake bisected horizontally by a line of pink jam. Ulises ordered cheesecake, and in a matter of minutes they were engaged in the civilized British ritual of afternoon tea.

"You are planning to execute Margaret Thatcher?" inquired the esteemed translator, as he dabbed his grey beard with a napkin. "You know," he whispered, "she is no longer in power."

José choked. "Shut up. Please. I don't want to get arrested." He ate quickly two forkfuls of cake. "Don't forget, we are foreigners here."

"The enemy, no less," grinned Pereira, licking his moustache.

"I am starting a new life. I do not need you."

Pereira guffawed.

José noticed the man's sharp eye teeth. "I will go to Spain once I have saved some money." Why was he being so forthright? He'd hoped to outrun this demon.

"Ah! To Barcelona, perhaps, where your father was planning on eloping with his communist girlfriend?"

José hurled the remains of his cake in Pereira's face. A security guard approached them. "Everything all right here, sir?"

José rose, smiling, avoiding the smashed, jammy cake bits goring up the floor. "Yes, absolutely. Just a little accident."

The security guard unclipped his walkie-talkie. "I'll get someone to clear that up for you."

World War II, World War I, the Crimea... he backtracked his way out of the building. But his pursuer had not been shaken off. Ulises was now grabbing José's briefcase while the sun struggled to come out over the Lambeth Road.

"Those are not your pictures, Pereira." He wrestled his briefcase away. Pereira was surprisingly strong, despite his parentheses of grey frizz and faint, flat-beer smell of age and uselessness. Perhaps the old man was not so old. Fifty-three: the age José's father would be if he had not been kidnapped and then tortured in some concentration camp housed in a sports stadium, a residential basement, a disused hospital, or maybe behind the door of an auto mechanics' shop within spitting distance of commuters on their way to work.

"Ah, yes, beautifully rendered."

Now seated on a bench, Pereira licked his index finger and was paging through José's illustration portfolio. His voice was measured, careful. "And with this, you hope to gain entrance to an art school, or else find work with a publisher of some sort." His finger came to rest on a page José did not recognize, a scrap of yellowing lined paper covered with an ugly ballpoint pen sketch of what appeared to be a male corpse. "Now, this is excellent. Quite macabre."

"I didn't draw it. What's it doing here?"

"This," smiled Pereira, "was your father's last doodle, scrawled it in his notebook the evening he disappeared."

José tried to stand but fell back onto the bench.

"Here, breathe into this," said Pereira, retrieving from a nearby garbage can a paper McDonald's bag. "Tell it your secrets. Go on. No one will hear."

The bag stank of cheese and ketchup.

Pereira's hands gripped the back of José's neck, crept around his throat, dug into his esophagus. "You let us down," he said. “We needed those islands.”

Then Pereira was gone, leaving the contents of José’s portfolio scattered on the grass. José tucked the yellow paper inside his pocket. He did not want it to blow away on an English wind. He would make his way to Spain as soon as possible.

III

José takes along his black silk scarf. For a moment, he thinks Alice won't show, but there she is, dressed in a mauve shirt, carrying a camera around her neck: the horse with red hair.

He takes her to the Metro. "Today you must trust me," he says.

"Where have I heard that before?" Alice snaps a picture of him before he can stop her, a man holding out a map. But the map is of Buenos Aires.

"What will happen if we use this to get where we are going?" he asks. It is a map from before the war. He found it in his father's bookshelves, tucked between Aristotle and Nietzsche. The streets it names may or may not exist today. The city has become a stranger to him.

"Where are we going?"

"Somewhere with a view."

When they get off the Metro he asks her to close her eyes. Then he spins her around, takes the scarf and ties it three times around her head. That she willingly consents to this baffles him. In London, he walked with his hands in his pockets, fists clenched, ready to start a fight. Alice's arms are at her sides. Her mouth is relaxed but shrewd, a red-painted beast. José remembers a game he played with friends as a child, looking at their faces upside-down until they became new faces, eyeless and bulging. Who is this woman he has blindfolded?

"I presume you know what you're doing," she says.

"Just take my hand. Sometimes we need to be imprisoned to understand our agency, or lack of it." If he has learned anything, it is this.

Slowly he guides her over the road. He notices on her behalf every bump along the way, the unexpected ridges that threaten to trip her. Together they navigate. It is like tango, this communication in the hands. He remembers his father speaking once of a blind guitar player whose hands could see everything, even the mistakes of other players. He could correct their posture, even their fingering. Carlos had never played music of any kind but was fascinated by it, a child who could watch an insect for an eternity, until the world faded away.

"What's this?" The funicular arrives and its doors wheeze open. She fumbles with the scarf. "I need to see."

"No," he says, gently pulling her hand away. "Trust me."

They take a seat. A family of three gets into the same compartment, a man, a woman and a small boy. The man looks pointedly at José. This could go wrong, he thinks. The man sits down next to his wife and pulls the boy onto his lap.

Once when José was a child, his mother took him on a blindfolded trip to the zoo. He remembers the sounds, the clunk of his feet on the bus steps, the rip of the paper ticket as they entered the zoo, and then the terrifying bellow and chatter of macaques. He nearly wet himself. He cried silently but refused to pull off the scarf until his mother asked, "Are you ready, José?"

"Yes, Mami."

The solid stink of feces that was half hay, half loneliness, the marble of an eye glinting with reflected light: he had always wanted to see an elephant, and his mother knew that this way he would really see it. The great creature in front of him, whole.

Alice pulls at the scarf. José touches her hand, stops her. "Are you ready, Alice from nowhere?"

The funicular stops, the doors wheeze wide and the cool air of the mountaintop wraps around them. A distant tinkle of what sounds like fairground music. José guides her to the gate and pays for them both before she finally gets her bearings.

A balding man is grinning at him, giving him the thumbs up. They continue. He notices two young women giggling nervously, pointing at Alice, whose head rotates from side to side, trying to source the sound.

"I know where we are," she says after a few minutes. "I've read about about this fair. Take me back. I can't stand fairground rides. Can we go back, or at least can I take off this damned scarf?"

"No," he says. She is laughing, her fear is palpable. She clenches her camera in both hands, the game still on.

"You will be able to take your pictures soon."

He guides her slowly, dodging small children and itinerant ice cream sellers, past the pony ride and the Western-style Rio Grande train that rolls past plaster cacti and cowboys who lurk behind rocks. He continues until they reach their destination: the gaudy, swinging capsule of the Talaia, lifting, pausing and falling on its endless circuit, up into the thin air above the mountain and down again to the ground.

They are second in line. A dreamy-looking couple get on first, gazing into each other's eyes as a tired-looking boy closes the gate behind them. Alice fidgets. She is finished with this game, but attempts to wait like a French aristocrat before the guillotine, making peace with a cruel god. Up goes the Talaia, hovering at its zenith.

"Get ready," says José, his mouth so close to Alice's ear he could bite it. "It's almost our turn."

The ride is swinging down. Down come the couple, their hands grasping the cold metal bar that holds them in. The boy in the red shirt unlocks the gate.

Up, up they rise, into the cool air, the little space they stand in swinging slowly sideways as the long arm of the Talaia lifts them up.

The cart swings to and fro, nudged by the wind. "Now," says José, spinning Alice around and untying at last the black silk scarf to reveal to her the whole world.

She grimaces, opens her eyes, squints. The day is an expanse of light and space. Before them sits the lonely church of the Sagrat Cor, from which a giant Christ rises and opens his arms to the sea.

Already they are beginning their slow fall back to earth.

"Take a photograph," José says.

She lifts her camera to her right eye, observes, snaps the shutter. José reaches out his hand.

"Let me take one of you."

José will not hurt this woman, nor will he let her hurt him. But even simple theft has its consequences. Alice passes him the Nikon and he raises it to his eye, pretends to shoot, then tosses it over the edge and out into history, out beyond them, into the crystalline air.

❧

She does not speak to him on the way back into town. She runs her fingers over the cracked case and lens cap of her camera—a tour guide had picked up its pieces and placed them in a plastic bag. José sits opposite, watches her for signs of a shifting mood. As soon as they arrive, she leaves without a word.

He lies awake that night, shaking with anger. He curses and spits, he presses his face into the sheets. It's not the end. How can it be? He still has a piece of her. And she, presumably, still has a piece of him.

The following week, he calls to apologize, they speak slowly together for over an hour. They agree to see a movie—terrible—*Evita,* starring Madonna, and afterwards, over coffee, he does his best to educate her about his country and how unromantic, in his opinion, it actually is.

"Unless you find cows sexy," he says. "There are very many of them." He draws a sketch of two cattle dancing tango, and titles it "El Amor" *Fileteado*-style. "Someone should make a musical about your Margaret Thatcher, perhaps—her life, her loves, her handbags," he says, thinking of the so-called Iron Lady, a Joan Rivers doll cast in steel. Sometimes Thatcher looks a bit like the Statue of Liberty and sometimes more like his mother. He really has no idea who she is, just as Alice has no idea about Perón. Their worlds are cartoons. No wonder they cannot communicate, not in English, not in the dark. A secret lies between them.

After the movie, Alice goes back to her hotel and he collapses in a fit of doubt. Shivering for a moment on his apartment balcony, he looks at his reflection in the half-open French door: a loner with too much gel in his hair. He humiliated her, and yet she's still interested. He throws his cigarette butt over the railing.

That night in his dream Alice cuts her own cheek with an army knife. There is no blood. He takes the knife in his hand and it turns into a calligraphy pen. He attempts to write an urgent love letter to her, but the pen bends and collapses.

"Do you ever forget things?" he asks, attempting to put a meal together, of rice, prawns, onions, garlic and tomatoes. She is back in his kitchen in white jeans and a yellow top that does not match her hair. He does not know exactly what he is asking.

"Your name? Your age? Your address?" He slides the chopped vegetables into the frying pan and the hot oil spatters his shirt. There's no way she's as fucked in the head as he is. Nevertheless, he's genuinely curious.

"Sometimes I wake up. In the middle of the day. It could be in the city or at work. I will suddenly open my eyes not knowing how I got to where I am. This has always happened to me. Even as a child, words would come out my mouth, I was speaking French—I was very good at languages—some nonsensical words." As she talks, she braids and unbraids her hair. She is like Carlos, he thinks. Something about the smashed camera has opened her up to him.

He adds a handful of cayenne, a twist of black pepper. Turns the heat down and opens a bottle of fragrant Gewürztraminer.

Words come out of her mouth. Her name is Jane: just Jane. Not Alice. And her surname isn't Barrow, but Shaw. Perhaps, if he's patient, more will be revealed. He can feel the balance between them shifting.

"Cheers," he clinks her glass, his hand unsteady. "Salud." He's standing, she's sitting. He gulps down his wine. "Tell me about your family."

"Honestly, there's nothing to say." Plain Jane Shaw. She smiles. They are two dots on a screen, surrounded by millions of other dots. Separate, they mean nothing, but together they form a pattern, an implied line.

"Come on, of course there is. Your brother…"

"My brother, Peter." She lowers her head, places the

wineglass on the table. "The photographer." She laughs.

How long will this game go on?

The risotto is ready. He turns off the stove. Calmly spoons out two platefuls, garnishes them with slices of lemon and parsley. Serves her. Sits down.

"How about you go first," she says. "Tell me a story about your mother or father."

"My father..." How to speak of such absence?

"We have no records, I'm afraid," the kind but distant professor of European languages had confessed, when José visited the university his first week in Barcelona, eager to recover some news about Carlos. "That was several years ago. We don't hold onto our conference programs. But I can assure you if there had been any unusual correspondence the secretary would have filed it here." She had rifled through a manila folder dated 1977-78.

"He was a translator," José had said. "He was interested in languages. The challenge of translating the untranslatable." The woman nodded. "He wanted to change the Spanish language, our language..."

Jane takes his fork from his hand.

"Come to bed."

"If I could draw you," he says. But she has already pulled him away.

What is seen: ruddy strands of hair, darkened with sweat, against the forehead, skin the bluish colour of skim milk, a fading bruise, stippled purple, a shining scar, the flutter of an eyelid, arch of a spine, the cage of arms.

After they make love, Jane expertly rolls a joint, sprinkles chocolatey crumbs of hash into the tobacco and licks up the paper as if performing some sort of sublunary magic. José breaks his rule of no mind-altering substances one cannot sip from a glass, and inhales deeply, too deeply. His cough makes her laugh. He goes out onto the balcony and observes the city, as beautiful as ever, the peculiarities of its skyline familiar now as the profile of a lover. He traces its outline reluctantly with his hand.

Alice calls to him. "Now I've found you, I don't think I want to leave you." For a moment, he thinks she is talking about the city.

A hand presses into his shoulder. It is not hers. Already the solid outlines of the buildings are buckling. Water flows down from the top of the glass door of the balcony and floods the street. He grips the railing. The Malvinas are coming into view: his country's swarming multitudes, the future, the future, the future. The past.

José and Jane lie on the sand and stare at an ink-wet sky. They have spent the afternoon eating seafood and drinking beer in Barceloneta. Swimmers and their towels disappear from the beach.

"Ever since I discovered my brother's war trophies, I've been on a mission to find you." She sits up, hugs her knees. "Five years ago, I wrote to the Argentinian embassy in London. They said they could do nothing. But some chap recognized you—or thought he did—some translator. Javier Martínes."

"Javier."

"Yes."

"Jesus Christ."

"So, I went to see him. He made a few phone calls, told me—if you were who he thought you were—that you were either dead or no longer in Argentina."

"Did he give you my name?"

"No. Well, not at first. But then he did some digging."

"And so, you came here?"

"Not at first. I decided to wait. And anyway, I didn't know where you were. But then, after Greece, I decided to come to Spain. I knew there were lots of expats here, and then I saw the poster for your exhibit."

"Oh. That?" His exhibition had been so lightly received, he had almost forgotten about it. "That was almost a year ago." A small selection of his postwar sketches, displayed in a little gallery his ex-girlfriend Elena had worked at. Only one sold: an eccentric nude. The poster Elena designed still hung in his hallway.

"That's how I knew you were here."

"So what do you want? You're going to take another picture?" He stands up, shivering in the breezy twilight. "Get yourself another little souvenir?" He kicks the sand.

"No." Jane stands, puts on her sandals. "I don't know what I want. I'm sorry." She wraps her sweater around her. "It was selfish. I wanted to understand my brother, I guess." The sky behind them is pale green. "But I see now I can't."

He hasn't painted for a long time. But he needs something to do, something to stop himself from talking, so he buys a basic set of acrylics and mixes them up on old cardboard, throws together layers of coral, emerald, ochre and scarlet, leans the large canvases up against walls and simply leaves them there as if to make the apartment disappear. She sits behind him while he paints.

"Why don't you try?"

"Okay," she says, but applies the paint to tattoo her arms, her legs and torso, in purple, white, and red. Afterwards, when they are together in the shower, he watches the colours mix and become a dull grey. The grey of winter.

❦

The longer she stays, the harder it is for him to focus. They smoke and drink and fuck and laugh. Gaudí's crazy buildings begin to play tricks on him, rippling like cloth in a breeze. He can imagine their maker, a haunted fellow in a black hat and moustache, fruitlessly trying to cross an empty road. Then Miguel appears, a long dark shadow luxuriating in the shuttered doorway of a *pastelería*, turning high-heeled pumps over in his hands.

One day he will just give up, unzip the fat, navy blue sports bag he keeps his mother's letters in, lift it up, and tip it out over the bed.

"I don't feel well," he says. They are standing on the balcony.

She touches his face.

"I left all my clothes," she says, "and my jewellery. I got up and walked out through the Plaka and got on the bus without even washing my face. I had my money, my sterling. That was all.

"I made a mistake. I thought I could live like a girl I once knew, a barmaid who had a boyfriend who barely spoke, and I thought how wonderful to not have to speak. Just to live, to experience, you know, each day, just like that, no past, no future. But it didn't work, using someone as an escape hatch. I've wasted half my twenties, running away."

She takes a drag, closes her eyes. He's collapsing.

"If I was my city," he says, attempting to distract himself, "I would be covered in tattoos." He goes inside. Jane follows. He picks up some paper and a Biro, that marvellous device invented by an Argentine, and begins to make circles, dark blue, cutting through the page. "After the dictatorship, someone began to draw silhouettes on the walls. Nobody knew who. The pictures just appeared overnight, the outlines of people with empty insides, like the shadows left on buildings after Hiroshima. This was in the early years, before people spoke. Words had been contaminated—they poisoned people's mouths. There was no way to talk about what was no longer there and yet was more present than their own bodies—the holes in the street, the noises coming from the Athletic Club, the mouths of those who never intended to leave—and so everyone forgot to speak.

"As part of the tenth anniversary celebrations of the fall of Videla, so my mother says, there were canvases placed on either side along the Avenida de Mayo which the artists named a bridge of remembrance. I wish I could have seen them. I wish I could have crossed that bridge, but my compatriots have rejected me—a coward. I returned to their city defeated, a broken man, and there was no victory parade. Some of us were scorned and spat at. We were the losers who had caused our nation such shame and now that nation was disintegrating.

"The canvases were all destroyed. But my mother can walk there. She is friends with some of the other mothers. The army chief of staff has apologized. The lists of names have been published. What more could a wife want? It is time to move on. We have other problems now, economic and colonial. We are an industrialized country with no true society, just the charred remains of the bones of others on which we build our cathedrals, our shopping malls. As if we had vanquished death."

He goes to the bedroom and takes out the photograph of the children he has carried all these years. "Is this you?"

Jane's mouth falls open. "Where on earth did you get it?" Her eyes harden, dart between him and the photograph, in apparent disbelief.

"It appears I stole it from your brother on the SS *Uganda* in 1982."

His mouth tastes foul. He is hungry, starving. The world is bleached and taking on the reversed tones of a photographic negative, all its shadows turning into light.

Jane's voice is quiet. "He took this with him."

"Yes."

"And you've waited this long to show me?"

He looks away. "Does he know you're here?"

"Of course not." She pauses. "We don't talk."

"I think you should take it." Better late than never. All he wants now is to surrender, to let those children go and see what comes back.

❧

"After he joined up, I hated him," she says, in the dark. "Hated what he stood for. All that warmongering. How he postured. For a while I lived at a peace camp. He was injured, as you know, but he came back alive. Made it out still believing in queen and country. He thought what they did was right. Still does."

"And he brought back my picture." He sits up, rigid. His stomach muscles tighten. "An act of shame."

"It haunted me. I'm sorry. I didn't expect this."

The darkness is physical. A density of absence.

❧

The next day he takes her to Portlligat and the Salvador Dalí House. She brings a disposable camera and takes pictures while José sketches people and dogs all the way there and back. The dogs look like people, and the people look like dogs. In the whitewashed garden, he takes her picture. Inside, he rears up like Dalí's stuffed polar bear. Together they peer into the centre of a giant cracked egg.

"Was Dalí mad?" she asks.

"No, he was an excellent businessman."

Later that night they finish the remains of a lasagna and drink the last of the wine and go to bed. After they make love, José gets up and stumbles to the bathroom. He turns around to see she has followed him, a strange, pale shape.

"Would you come back to England with me?" She has wrapped the sheet around her naked body. "We could…"

"No." The word exits like a bullet.

Jane steps back. He is irritated. He retreats to the kitchen and opens another bottle of wine. Jane joins him, still wrapped in the sheet. "We could start again." She blows her nose. Outside there is the sound of laughter, a party just starting up in the street. Inside, the air is heavy. José senses his own depth, his unbroken permafrost.

"Rosa? Are you there?"

"Who is this?" A woman's voice, not his mother's.

"I am sorry. Is this the residence of Raúl García?"

"No, it is not!" The woman slams down the receiver. José calls back and this time the woman explains that Rosa has moved out. She, Maria, has been living with Raúl for six months already.

"For a while, I was getting all her calls. Here is her new number," she tells him.

He gets a strange, recorded message: *Good day, you have reached the residence of Señor Benicio Salgado. Please leave a message after the beep.*

Salgado—the name is familiar, and not in a good way. Feverish, he grips the side of the bed. Restless in her grief, she has left Raúl and taken up with a tango-dancing entrepreneur.

He dimly recalls a letter that explained her sudden departure from Raúl. The alarm clock reads 2:45 AM.

"José," Rosa says two days later, when he finally gets through. "Things are different. You can start again."

He hangs up, wanders into the hallway as Jane sleeps. Her red purse hangs on a hook beside her denim jacket. He opens it. A copy of Plath's *Ariel*, a dog-eared book in Greek, several Tampax, a bunch of change. And a business card. *Peter Shaw: Weddings, Portraits.* A date and time on the back of it: *March 6, 8:25 PM.*

He slips the card into the pocket of his own jacket, hanging on the hook beside hers. He goes back to bed. Later, in the dark, he reaches for her, feels the heat beneath her skin. There's a passion there, a fire that could thaw him completely.

Papi, he prays. *Miguel.* But he's stuck with the living.

"What are you thinking about?" she whispers, awakened by his hand.

"Nothing," he says.

IV

The day Peter finally comes home, there's a Union Jack in the window. Jane has refused to travel to Southampton, where the jingoistic fervour is at its height, and stays in her room instead, waiting for his return. They've a special tea ready—Mum's lamb curry, plus a rhubarb crumble. In his letters, Peter said he'd been missing custard.

In the long hours before he arrives, she chops off her hair. Now it's spiky and black, not reddish and curly. When she sees her brother, her heart stops. *He could have died.* She grabs him, hugs him, then pulls back to look at the limping whole of him—Peter, the lumbering miscreant.

"What the fuck did you do to your bloody hair?"

❧

It's only later, days later, that she hears him describing the exhilaration of battle. "An incredible high. Even when I was crapping myself." He wants to go back, but his injury means a desk job unless he can somehow return to his former fitness level. He has a metal rod in his leg now. "Like the Bionic Man."

"What about photography?" It's her mother speaking. Jane

leans in to listen from her place in the kitchen. They think she's studying. They think she's a bloody nutcase. Unpatriotic.

There's a strange silence. "Mum, Dad, fancy a cup of tea?"

❦

The photographs were in an envelope, along with their negatives. Most were of the journey out. But three or four were clearly of the battlefield. She slid them out of the envelope, careful to only touch their edges. He didn't know she was in there. She had to be quick.

The man in the picture looked dead, except for his eyes, which were half-open. His head, tilted to one side, belonged to a young man. A man as young as she was. Her eyes burned. Her throat began closing up.

There was a number, barely visible, on the soldier's epaulette. Jane squinted at it.

She took the photo with her on the bus to Athens, that one photograph, tucked inside an Indian embroidered purse. After her arrest at a protest against Cruise missiles, after Peter started drinking too much and refusing to talk, her parents had disowned her. Perhaps, if she ever returned, they would tell her they missed her.

V

José stays in Barcelona until winter. He visits Madrid and Seville, takes a train north to Paris, where he sleeps overnight on a bench in the Gare du Nord, and decides, upon finishing his last cigarette, to keep going. The tunnel to London is not yet finished, so he travels to Calais and takes the boat.

The ferry bar is filled with cigarette smoke and abandoned newspapers. It's Major now who's responsible for the deaths of young soldiers; no one seems to like him very much, a dull grey man destined to be forgettable, which perhaps makes him more dangerous.

Eventually the houses of outer London roll past the train window, those quilted fields he's admired in movies when women in bonnets and men with crooks scurry along narrow lanes before the camera swoops down to alter their lives. The man across from José coughs into his Guardian. A packet of dry-looking sandwiches with the clear plastic wrapping half peeled off sits on the seat beside him. José looks down at the sandwich then up to the window glass, where his face and upper body are reflected, sees only an X-ray, an image of shadow and bones.

They are passing through a tunnel. The man takes a bite of a sandwich. José rifles in his pocket for a tube of mints. He recalls his missing boots. Perhaps today he will win them back. His right foot burns. A cold strip of webbing constricts his heart.

The train stops. He disembarks, and finds his way to a different platform, where he takes a smaller, local train. Inside, the upholstery has been slashed and there is graffiti on the wooden doors. When the train stops again, the houses do not look poor. They are small but elegant. He visits the toilet and regards himself in the dirty mirror whose screws have rusted, spreading blood-like speckles across the glass. Dark, greying hair, a two-day beard, open-necked polo shirt and crumpled beige slacks. Even in his new clothes he is identifiable. As clearly as if he were wearing an army-issue parka.

In the village he finds a phone booth. The glassed-in box smells of urine. He dials the number from the business card, and as usual gets the answering machine. On the other end: silence. The receiver is heavy in his hand.

He walks past a stone obelisk decorated with a variety of aging wreaths, a park surrounded by orderly flower beds. He turns right and goes inside a small store. The elderly woman behind the counter is watching TV. She does not look as if she wants to be interrupted. He purchases a pack of cigarettes, a bar of chocolate and a can of cola. "Just turn left there," she says, pointing out the door to an indeterminate crossroad.

The office is joined to the house next door, their front yards divided by a high hedge. José walks by the house once and then returns. A small plastic truck lies on the front path. The yard is well tended. There is a row of pale pink begonias. On his second pass, he notices a tuft of brown fur snagged on a diminutive holly bush. He steps up to the office door, pushes through to a counter, rings the bell. A buxom woman with thick makeup appears behind the counter. "Do you have an appointment?" José wonders if she is the wife. On closer inspection, she's rather old. She stares.

He's left his luggage in a locker at the station and his watch does not look English. Nor do his shoes, even though he bought them here. "I would like to surprise my wife with a portrait of our dog." He is sweating. His legs are shaking.

"A pet portrait. Right." The woman smiles. Her teeth are disconcertingly perfect.

A man walks in, about José's age, heavier and taller. He is carrying a camera case on his shoulder. José looks up, and for a moment he is on the tundra.

"This gentleman is looking for a pet portrait."

"Is that right? Well, he's in the wrong place, isn't he?"

"No, no, actually you see..." José indicates his body, apologetically. "I am from Mexico."

"Mexico. Really." The woman's plucked eyebrows arch.

"And I have lost my passport." José pauses. "So you see, I need a new photograph, as soon as possible, so I can get back to my wife, and her dog, which is to say, our dog. Whose name is... how do you say this in English? *Licorice.*"

"Right, well, that's easily arranged." Mr. Shaw steps behind the counter. "Pass me the book, Brenda."

Brenda passes him a large black ledger. Her legs are long and bony in their stockings. José wonders if she once owned a red, pig-faced gas mask and had it strapped to her face.

"Well, you're in luck; it looks as if there's an opening. I'm usually booked on Tuesdays. It's my discount day." They are having him on.

José stands up tall. He is more successful than this man. Even though he lost the war. The Englishman slams the book shut. "Step through here, into the studio." He holds back a curtain. "It'll only take a few minutes." Peter Shaw's smile is perfunctory. José has yet to dare look him fully in the face.

A room that is not a room. A chair, a low table, a vase, backdrops and lights that together disguise the small dusty windowless place through which Shaw seems to move like both a janitor and a shaman, tidying and conjuring as he goes.

"Sit here." He places a high stool in front of a plain white wall. No waterfall or starry night for José, not even a fake location. José hoists up his pants and climbs onto the stool. Shaw turns to face him. José examines his skin. Tanned ruddy by the weak British sunlight, loosening a little around the jaws, pocked with enlarged pores. Peter did not shave this morning either. His shirt is white with a dim beige check: the sleeves rolled up, his forearms exposed, strong and muscular.

The camera on the tripod is not the Minolta, it is a Nikon. Shaw gets behind it, and José can't see his face anymore, just this one black eye through which he will gaze. José must not appear worried. Nor must he appear smug. A passport is a privilege. As is a name: *José Rinaldo Jorge Hector Ramírez.* He feels his mother poised behind him, his father looking out through his eyes.

"Lift your chin." José lifts it. "Down a little." He lowers it. "Turn your head to the right just a tad…" He moves his head. He thinks of the knife he brought, sharp enough to sever Peter Shaw's fingers. When should he step out from behind himself?

The camera clicks. Fires off a volley of muffled shots.

"That's great. You can relax now. Thank you, Mr.…."

"Mr. Ramírez."

Shaw steps out from behind the camera and for a moment José thinks he sees a twitch, an unconscious panic ripple across the man's face.

Shaw stands between him and the door. José could walk past his assistant and be at the station in five minutes. Better to jump into a cab, after he's throttled his enemy. Take the train to the airport and leave. There is a flight to Venezuela this evening, he checked before he left Heathrow. He is crawling out into the line of fire like a wolf-dog, about to be extinguished.

Trust me, says Pereira. *I will guide you.*

"Tell me, have we met before?"

"I don't think so."

José steps toward him. His pulse accelerates. *Close your eyes,* says the old man. *Let me lead the way.*

"If you'd care to wait outside, Mr. Ramírez," Shaw gestures through the door back into the waiting area, "I'll have these ready in a matter of minutes."

Now, watch.

José sees himself take another step forward, pressing Shaw to the wall. He places his hands on either side of the Englishman's head. He smells sweat, a hint of cheap cologne. Must be his wife who gave that to him. His wife, beautiful and ignorant, carrying his child over her shoulder, a boy of about three, dressed in a red and blue striped T-shirt. *Ask him if anyone in his family has ever been murdered.*

Shaw punches him in the gut, and as José staggers backwards, he crashes into the tripod and knocks over the camera. Pieces of plastic and glass fly. *That's right. That's how it should be.* José swings back and punches the Englishman in the face and slams him against the wall. Yes.

Around them is frozen tundra and the explosion of hand grenades. The Englishman leans into José's face and regards him so coldly it's as if he is a corpse. An anatomical sketch. Where is the tumour located? How does the bullet travel, from entry to exit and where will the blood loss be greatest?

Tell him you want your boots back.

"Everything okay there?" A hand lands on José's shoulder. "You look a little pale."

Tell him you want your soul back.

"The waiting room is this way."

Brenda hands José a polystyrene cup of milky tea. When the photos are ready, he leaves for the station. Across the street, a fox trots past, a dead kit hanging from its mouth.

The train up the Spanish coast eventually swings inland. As the sun goes down, the lights of France swing round from west to east; a distant fairground. Jane sits cross-legged in the corridor, smoking her last Spanish cigarettes. The air is warm and fragrant. Someone has opened the sash window, and guitar music judders out from inside one of the compartments.

Tomorrow, everything will be different. She will arrive back in England and start a new life, empty of desire, and there will be no more chasing after strangers. Tomorrow, or the day after, she will find out if she is carrying José's child.

He once spoke of the thousand fires of Tierra del Fuego, the lights the explorers saw from their incoming ships. He'd read about it in some book; he was always reading. For the past six years, Jane has hardly written. *I'll get back to my writing,* she thinks. *Eventually. Once I've decided what to do.*

It would have been better, he said, if they'd sailed away. Turned around, and taken that image with them; like coming upon a house already occupied, and leaving with just a memory of a candle in its window.

That's all very well, she retorted. *But they didn't, did they? They were never* not *going to land; not after that journey. Not with everything they believed in. You can't just…* Her hands whirled about, making empty, ridiculous gestures. How could anyone untangle cause and effect?

Instead of continuing to argue, José took her hands in his,

and laid them down firmly upon the table. Her palms ache for that reassuring pressure. She places her hand against her cheek, and for a moment it is not her own.

❧

When José takes himself to the forest, he's surprised by how thin the woods are, just a narrow belt of trees around a man-made lake, a motorway humming in the distance. This is where Jane said she would escape to, when she wanted her solitude. Today the rustling birch leaves are waxy with promise and a fleet of fresh juvenile swans eddies out on the lake. The path is reddish. A middle-aged couple walks with a little white dog. Unleashed, the dog runs into a copse, and José follows. Inside, the ground is marshy. Clumps of faded bluebells erupt here and there. José lies down, presses his face into the earth, puts out his tongue and tastes it: acrid and gritty. Opens his arms, widens his legs and stretches them into an X.

She told him that when she came she saw blue flowers. Always blue. "A shade you never see, though, I think it's invisible, or at least when I see it I know I'm not looking anymore."

After she left, he did not go to work for a week. Nor did he answer his phone. Eventually he admitted to himself the paradox at the centre: that he could not run any further without turning back. But neither did he want to get out from between the sheets. It was a sickness he had, and her pale, freckled skin was the medicine to reverse it. He knew he was shattered to his core.

After removing a picture of her Greek ex-husband, she had slid the childhood photograph into a pocket of her wallet. "Tell me about this guy," José had said, tapping the little blond boy.

"There's not much to tell," she said. "Just what I've already told you." Shaw was a war hero, a veteran who supported the government. After the war, he grew depressed and lost a few years to drink, but he was now married with a baby and the apple of their mother's jaundiced eye.

"He was funny. Kind. Used to be my very best friend. But he changed. We stopped spending time together. It was like we had a choice: be bad or be good. I chose the first and he chose the second."

"What kind of bad?"

"I ran away for a few months. Took drugs. Nothing too serious. Lived with a man who was later arrested for murder."

José put his hand on her shoulder, pulled her back to face him. "Did he hurt you?"

"No. He was a lamb. It's the good ones you have to watch out for."

"And why did you go back?"

"Home? I don't actually remember."

Between the bluebells, he plays dead. The bright clatter of songbirds up in the branches. Lying in the dirt he imagines Jane's lips; bitter and sweet. Then the little white dog is upon him, licking his face.

PART THREE

I

José arrives in Ezeiza to be met by Rosa, who has cut her hair short, its dark brown now streaked with blond. She looks fit and strong; not what he expects. He imagined a softer life would render her shapeless.

She hands him a box of cookies: *alfajores.* As if he is a tourist. "In celebration of your arrival," she says after she embraces him, determinedly wiping the tears from each eye: one, two. Her shirt is white and decorated with polka dots, and as they hug, he feels the muscles in her arms.

"You look more handsome than ever, my darling prodigal."

She's lying, of course. He has aged more than she has. But it's hard to know how to behave, or what to say. He has only one suitcase. She insists on carrying it herself, all the way to the car. The sun is bright, far too bright. New shanty towns have grown up, visible from the road.

After some initial chatter, they travel in silence. José feels strangely young. Did the past six years happen? Rosa tells him her news. She's working for a housing co-operative that will build a dedicated complex for the poor.

"I am looking forward," she says. "Always looking forward." She does not turn to him, even as she speaks. Not until they enter the centre of the city, where she pauses at a stoplight and aggressively pats his knee. Her eyes are bright, her smile tight. José feels thirteen. "I forgive you," she whispers. "I forgive you."

Rosa and Benny live in a new apartment complex in Recoleta. After parking the car in the underground lot, Rosa punches in the security code while José inhales French perfume and rotting leaves; once inside the flat, he does not recognize anything except for an old, framed photograph of the Congreso, which he remembered hung in the hallway of his childhood home. He fingers its gilt frame for a moment, then retracts his hand. Her home makes him feel dirty and he doesn't want to leave greasy fingerprints.

The walls and ceilings of the open-plan apartment are white, the furniture modern and mostly black, and through the window José can see one corner of the library, its coil of knowledge held tight above the barrio streets. He wants to visit. To go down on hands and knees and devour the stacks.

The calla lilies in the enormous purple glass vase are for him. Glossy fashion architecture magazines are set at forty-five degrees to each other on the glass-topped coffee table, and a large-screen TV dominates one wall. Rosa's off-white trench coat slides off her arm. She hangs it in the closet.

"Benicio is so excited to meet you."

José isn't sure where to sit down. Cautiously, he does a few side bends. His body is stiff. His shabby suitcase has been set down by the wall.

"I should give you this," says Rosa, reappearing in a pair of white sneakers. She hands him an envelope. He recognizes Gaby's handwriting.

"How long…"

"Years." Rosa's tone is sharp.

"Why didn't you forward it?" He tears open the envelope.

Inside, there is a short note and two photographs: Gaby's children. He turns to the letter. She is living in Corrientes. She invites him to reply, if he chooses, and lists her address. Her signature is exactly the same as he remembers it.

He stuffs the letter and photographs into his jacket pocket. He is already keen to run. But Rosa has produced fresh coffee. And pastries. Fancy ones, from a bakery. He feels sweaty and crumpled and would like a shower. Instead, he sits at the table as instructed and helps himself to a buttery *factura.* He discovers that he is very hungry, and eats too quickly. Just as he finishes his second pastry, Benicio appears.

"José." The stocky, well-muscled man takes him in an embrace. His cologne is pungent. As José steps back, he takes in the neatly-trimmed hair, the shining bald patch, and the smile, which is radiant, yet tender.

"Señor Salgado." The rich man; the entrepreneur.

"Benny, please. I am so, so happy to finally meet you. Sit. Please." Benny gestures to José and offers up the pastries, but José has lost his appetite. A sudden anger is knotting up his stomach.

"No, thank you. I'm full."

During the silence which follows, Salgado pours himself a cup of coffee. Rosa watches tensely from the kitchen. José wonders if they have planned this, this welcoming committee, and if so, how exactly it's supposed to end.

Benny tries again. "I know this must be difficult. You have been away a long time! But your mother was so excited to receive your phone call. She has told me many times what an intelligent man, what an outstanding artist you are..."

Really? Thinks José. *From what I recall, she had no opinion whatsoever.*

"Please, feel free to stay here as long as you like."

"Benny says he can find you a job," adds Rosa.

"Whoa," says José, pushing back abruptly from the table. The coffee cups rattle. His foot is stuck. He panics.

"Okay, okay," says Rosa. "We don't need to talk about everything right away..."

What does she mean? Her eyes are bright. "I'm sorry," he says. "I apologize." He'd like to say more. He is standing now, beside the table, relieved to see he is closer to the door than Benicio.

Rosa glances at Benny, then back at José. "You are tired. Let me show you to your room." Grateful, he follows Rosa down a hallway, then up some stairs to the second floor, where a stationary bicycle sits in the corner of a messy office; beside the office is the tiny blue-painted bedroom Rosa says is for him. Inside, there's a double bed with brand new bedding. A Boca Juniors poster on the wall.

"Thank you, Mami." José's voice catches. He mustn't cry.

He tests the mattress: firm. Lies down and tries to rest, but the room is too empty. He can already see its corners filling with ghosts. If he spends the night here, he will end up bashing his head against the walls.

11

The shoe store is still recognizable, although it has been converted into a cut-price fashion retail outlet. He isn't sure why he has come here, other than Miguel would be glad.

He flips absently through a rack of dresses before asking the young sales clerk casually about Inés and Vicky. He is told brusquely that Inés has just stepped out. He goes outside and smokes, paces back and forth, trying to avoid the shop window. He's aware he appears agitated, and the last thing he needs is for the young woman to call the police.

When Inés arrives, he recognizes her immediately. Petite and dark, she still has the same determined walk. After kissing him liberally on both cheeks, she informs José that she held onto the lease, without telling her ex-husband, and took over again from the interim owners three years ago. "The smartest thing I ever did, short of getting my tubes tied." Inés wears wooden beads around her neck and wrist. She is no longer a practicing Catholic, she explains, but a "kind of Buddhist."

"I can't believe you recognized me," says José.

"Don't be ridiculous. Come upstairs for a minute. I can leave the store with Jacqueline."

The flat is filled with Buddhist icons. Inés tells José she

meditates up to two hours each day, which seems a lot for a "kind of" anything. When she offers him her room to stay in, he jokes that she will try to convert him. Her Catholic proselytizing is hard to forget.

"Don't worry," she says, "you are safe with me. I am not an evangelist any longer."

He laughs, although he still has his guard up. Like everyone else he has met so far, it will take some time to get used to this new version of her.

"How is it here, these days?"

"It's not that different, really. Now we just fear the peso, instead of the junta. The new president is such a hypocrite. I tell you, my sweet Alejandro would have loved him. Alejo, my dear man of God." Her black hair is now shot through with silver and her face has softened with age. Looking at her, José wonders what Miguel would have looked like, if he'd lived, then crushes that thought. Instead, he decides to take Inés up on her offer, and calls his mother to let her know he will not be back—at least not for a while.

"What about dinner, at least? Tonight, or tomorrow?" pleads Rosa.

"Next week."

"Okay." She pauses. "Do you have enough money?"

"Enough for now."

"Well, that's good, then, Josito." He's hurting her, he knows. "Take good care of yourself. Don't say we didn't try."

A week later, he is no closer to finding a job. The city is making money. The city is rebuilding itself. Analyzing itself, confessing, just a little. *Never Again* says the report, collected between covers. José reads it in pieces, standing in a bookstore, desperate to find some reference to Carlos, which he does not. On his way to and from the shoe store, José notices men sleeping in doorways, sleeping in blankets, their caps left out for change. Men of his age, veterans, who cannot reintegrate. Men who have split in two, just like himself. He remembers the helmet they used for maté, in the Malvinas, filled with pungent herbs. He might as well have kept one, for collecting change.

In the flat, he spends too much time looking through an album of old family photographs: Miguel, Vicky and Inés as children. That, and fitfully sleeping. He has not brought much with him. Five years in Europe and here he is, almost as poor as the day he left. He has shredded most of his work or given it away. His missing middle finger still throbs. He is desperate for distraction. Inés is good-looking in an austere sort of way. She makes it clear she is not interested in sex. Very nobly, she lets him sleep in her bed while she sleeps on a yoga mat in the living room. But only, she stresses, until she has had enough.

❧

"A man called Eduardo came around once," she says one Saturday morning. "He said he was in the war with you. You and Miguel."

They are in the living room smoking a joint. It helps lessen the pain in José's hands.

"He hadn't heard about Miguel."

"Eduardo." The little shit who reported him to Vargas. José exhales, slowly. *Stay calm.* "And how is he doing?"

"He wanted to invite you both to his wedding."

"Ha!" Bitterness in the throat. "Congratulations." Please, he begs silently of Inés, say no more.

"Miguel would have made a lousy husband." Inés raises her

eyebrows. It's a relief to hear her speak her brother's name. "He couldn't even sell shoes without flirting with every customer. And I mean every customer."

"This Eduardo," he persists. "Where exactly is he living?"

"San Antonio. With his lovely wife." Inés takes José's hand. "Perhaps you should meet up with some of your old comrades."

"Why?"

"It might help you to talk."

So that's it, thinks José. She wants to rescue me. Put me in touch with all the other sad fucks. He shakes off her hand. "I'm not interested in reliving the good old days. I'm interested in the future."

Which is, of course, bullshit. He gags, suddenly remembering a conscript he'd forgotten, also from San Antonio. Luis. A big, grain-fed lad. Always talking about the money he would make when he finally got home and took over breeding cattle. Less than a week after they arrived, Luis got caught in crossfire, and José was ordered to load him onto a stretcher. Luis's brain seeped out of a hole in his skull, like grey paste.

Later that afternoon, he borrows an oversized jacket from Inés and walks through the cemetery on his way to Rosa's flat. He has only visited the cemetery once, on a school field trip, back when he was young enough to wear an apron. He remembers hiding in an open vault, and jumping out at one of his schoolmates, who screamed and ran. Chill air, the clean smell of flowers mixed with a kind of rottenness. After the teacher had spanked him for his mischief, they all lined up to pay their respects to Eva. Remembering the trellised iron gate of her family vault, woven with red and pink roses, José thinks of his blond-haired grandmother in the provinces, who prays to Santa Evita every night.

Today, the city of the dead is sharply sunlit, its geometric streets empty of visitors, except for a small tour group several blocks ahead. As José comes up behind them, he hears a male voice tell the apocryphal story of the girl who was buried alive in her family vault.

"Her face and hands were scratched, and the coffin lid open… but it was too late. She had died once again of shock." The tour guide is speaking English. José stands quietly at the edge of the group. The guide is a boy: nineteen or twenty, a university student, José guesses, with an underused talent for drama.

"Oh my God! That is so *creepy*," says a woman in a bright pink beret. From the pitch of her voice, José guesses she is flirting with the boy, whose smile looks strained. The woman is decades older than the guide. Looking up, the guide catches sight of José, who nods reassurance. A fellow countryman. The guide waves. Is José being asked to leave, or join in?

"Now, over here…" The guide returns his attention to the group, leads them over to another famous, tragic statue, that of the fated gravedigger, David Alleno. José remembers this story, too.

I am a ghost among ghosts, he thinks. As the group moves off, he fights a sudden urge to yell. *You think that's creepy. Listen to this.* Then one of the Americans approaches, touches his arm.

"My apologies." The man retracts his hand. He's about Rosa's age, with curly grey hair. "I'm just wondering… Do you speak English?"

"Yes." It's a relief to speak. A reminder that he is still a living man.

The American lowers his voice. José notices he carries a walking stick: polished wood, with a bird's head for a handle.

"Do you think it's true? About the dead girl? I always like to get a second opinion."

"Absolutely," José replies. "And that is why you must always make sure your coffin has an escape hatch."

"Listen, my coffin *is* my escape hatch." The American laughs for a little too long then waves his walking stick around in the humid air.

❦

A thunderous rain begins. José takes cover under an Italianate gazebo, surrounded by bosomy, grieving angels. He closes his eyes and snow falls. He thrashes through it, claws his way up the ridge and back out through the gate just as it is about to close. A beggar sings out in the plaza. *Lucky saints' hair! Lucky saints' hair!* José tosses him two pesos but declines the relics. He no longer believes in Jesus Christ.

Still not ready, he finds a café and orders a Quilmes. Then another. Watches the soccer and the news without listening closely. Rosa and Benny invited him to accompany them tonight to a restaurant just down the street from their place. He has insisted his resistance to staying there has nothing to do with Benny. He's afraid to dislike the man and afraid to like him. Afraid there is nothing left of his father. Nothing left of himself.

It's suddenly far too late to go back to their place. He might as well go straight to the restaurant. Crossing Avenida Pueyrredón, he brushes lint off the jacket and straightens his collar. The restaurant is beautiful and oddly quiet, high-ceilinged, chandeliers, its panelled walls decorated with large colonial era war landscapes. To dine in here is to deny defeat. Benny is already waiting. His embrace is crushing.

He shows José a large corner table beside which a bottle of champagne is already chilling.

"Your mother is just in the washroom." His cufflinks are gold-plated cubes.

"Of course."

"José. Please. Order anything you like." José's fingers shake as he grips a glass of mineral water.

"Thank you, Señor Salgado."

"Benny, please. Remember?"

A waiter appears, pours the champagne. A basket of fresh bread appears, a platter of cheeses. Rosa slides into her seat and grasps Benny's hand. "We are so happy you are here, José," she announces. Her lipstick ghosts her glass.

Rosa orders fish. Benny orders a Milanese. José orders steak. It bleeds tenderly onto his plate.

"More wine?"

"Thank you." His edges blur. He expands into the victorious blue of the delta.

"We are going to dance afterwards. It is our little habit these days." Rosa glances at Benny then asks, "Would you care to join us?"

"Dance?" José does not understand the word.

"Yes," says Rosa. "Did you know that's where we met?" José has not considered the possibilities. "We danced for a year before we asked each other any questions."

"Where is this dance?"

"In Caballito."

Benny leans forward. "We would like to think it is not only old people like ourselves who enjoy the tango."

José smiles, briefly. "Did Papi dance?"

"He tried," says Rosa. "But mostly he preferred to watch."

No one raises the topic of José's future. They take a cab to the dance hall, the wet sidewalk glossy with puddles that Rosa steps over and José walks through. He doesn't have his dancing shoes on. Benny pays the entrance fees, and José wonders if the man ever wanted sons of his own.

The dance hall is only half full. Couples and small groups gather by the tables set around the dance floor, and Benny and Rosa move among them, kissing and being kissed. The floor is almost empty, except for an elderly couple who move together like lamé-clad martial artists engaged in a tense and subtle conversation of the musculature which hints at death, orgasm and spiritual enlightenment, all while involving little more than a rhythmic walk. Tango. The sport José's grandmother taught him, strutting around the dry grass of their yard at night in midsummer, her breasts at his ears, while his grandfather placed the heavy records on the record player and lowered its needle like a surgeon, dispassionate and exact.

José recognizes a few of the arrangements. D'Arienzo. Pugliese. He wishes he had better shoes, shoes for dancing, although he knows only the most basic steps: the walk, a few holds, simple ochos. It would be nice to hold a woman, to feel her hands upon his arms, her breath at his neck. But she would have to trust him, and he in turn would have to trust her.

He orders a bottle of wine to share. The waitress has a scar on her left cheek. After they have done their rounds, Rosa and Benny join him at the little table. Half past eleven, and the floor is now a slow kaleidoscope of recombining couples, a mosaic of red, blue and black dresses, silver and gold shoes, thin and thick ankles and grey, blond, brown and black hair. Watching the whole organism move makes José jealous, for in their circuits, performed to music composed during years of regret, which have themselves now vanished into history, the dancers appear to outfox aggression so nimbly that death is overcome for the duration of each song. Perhaps that's what they should have done in the Malvinas: milonga'd and Piazzolla'd their way through each confrontation; all the damn Brits had two left feet.

A waltz begins. Benny looks at Rosa, nods his head. She accepts and they stand to confront each other for a moment before Rosa places her hands on his hip and shoulder and he extends his foot behind him. Rosa extends hers forward. José massages his stiff neck, desperate for a cigarette. Good God, will he be stuck here all night, watching finely clothed hominids engage in this strange mating ritual? *Excuse me, I want to rape you. No, I don't think so. Well, why don't we just play pretend. How long can you hold it? Several hours. Too long. I'm impatient. I want to kill you. Well I want to kill you too. But not fast, slowly, so I can enjoy it. Fuck me. No. Trust me. Why should I? Just relax. Please. Close your eyes. Don't worry. Your gun is loaded. Your ejaculation is imminent. I can feel your buttocks clench. I can feel your teeth.*

José. José.

It's his old friend, Pereira, interrupting his daydream. *You have come back to face me. Care to dance?*

"Excuse me, is anyone sitting here?" A handsome older man hovers above him. Relieved to see it's not Pereira, José stands and offers one of the empty chairs.

The music becomes melancholy: controlled grief spiked through with sweet regret. The two-four rhythm, with its syncopated catch, hooks José in the diaphragm and he clutches his stomach, looks over the dance floor to where Rosa's right foot hovers, crosses back, reverses again as Benny suspends them both over the crevasse of the past. *José,* whispers Pereira. *José, I am waiting for you. Just give me time.* His mother and Benny have their eyes closed, they navigate by intuition, Rosa with the extended proprioception of the mortally wounded, Benny with the faith of the barely betrayed, and by the time José returns his focus to the table, to the chairs and the half-empty wine glasses, the old man has fallen completely asleep.

III

It's not easy to find work. In a moment of inattention, José mentions the war as the reason for his missing finger, and the medical textbook editor's face darkens. The interview is over. Walking past the green tents erected in the Plaza de Mayo, he turns up his collar. The veterans there are protesting, demanding government recognition, but José does not want to be recognized.

One day he walks the trains, looking for faces he knows, yet when he finds one—Señora Russo, his old mathematics teacher, asleep over a mystery novel—he breaks out in a sweat and turns away.

Adrift and resisting connection, he spends too much time on the streets until Inés eventually finds him a temporary position loading packages of meat into a giant freezer. At night the streets are filled with idle youngsters. He pushes through them, unlocks the back door and enters the building, where he strips off his jacket and pulls on his apron and gloves. He works alongside a deaf man named Enrico, a veteran of the factory night shift, whose animated signing he cannot understand. Enrico shows him where the meat is delivered and how to most efficiently load a dolly. The freezer has a combination lock. They work in silence for seven hours, stopping for washroom breaks and cigarettes. Sometimes, if he's just visited his mother, Enrico leaves José a portion of cold spaghetti to eat. Enrico's metal container is reminiscent of army mess tins. By the time their shift ends, the sun is already picking out shattered glass shards along the alley.

One night, three weeks in, Enrico doesn't show up. No explanation. Alone with the meat, José becomes increasingly afraid of the freezer, afraid he will inadvertently lock himself in. The packages of sausages collide as he piles them higher. The frozen blood of the ground beef reminds him of day-old corpses, their exposed flesh turned solid by sub-zero winds. He struggles to wheel the extra load into the hallway, down the bulb-lit corridor, and toward the freezer, which hums at him ominously.

You just aren't cut out for this, are you? José ignores the taunt and grasps the combination lock with the special grip he's developed, which allows him to work it with only his left hand.

Come on, son. Admit defeat. José heaves open the heavy door. Inside, propped on a shelf of lamb steaks, Ulises Pereira's head grins back at him, icicle-mustachioed.

Perhaps you should just crawl inside here and fall asleep.

José wakes to discover two days have passed. He's stretched out across Inés's bed, fully dressed, still wearing his apron. His mouth tastes terrible; he has a cut above his left eyebrow. A cold cup of coffee sits on the bedside table. The clock reads 2:43 PM, February 25.

José sits up and peels off first the foul-smelling apron, then his sweaty pants. He feels unsteady. There's a gnat-like whine in his ears. He staggers into the bathroom, gulps cold water from the tap, then gets into the shower. Hot. Scalding his back.

Inés calls up. "José? You are there?"

He shuts off the shower, pulls on clean jeans and a t-shirt, runs fingers through sopping hair.

He can't live here. She's getting to know too much. Soon she'll drag him to a doctor, or perhaps even a hospital. But she's kind. She doesn't ask questions. Or at least not the kind that would usually send him running.

"Jesus Christ. I thought you had gone."

He remembers. Rosa is taking the dogs to the vet today. She promised she would meet José for lunch. There is a sucking sound, as of organs slipping back and forth against each other. José senses Pereira somewhere behind him. Meanwhile, Inés stares up at him from the bottom of the stairs.

"Are you all right?" she asks, slightly irritated.

"Yes. I am fine. Although I missed my shift."

"You lost your job! Señor Marco phoned. You left the freezer open. Half of the meat was ruined. He wants you to pay him. I did my best to argue, but he wouldn't listen." She sighs. "I didn't know you were like this."

"Like what?"

"Like they say." She gestures roughly. "All messed up in the head."

His fists tighten. He must have used them recently: one knuckle is bruised. He descends the stairs. Inés hugs him but he doesn't feel much. They go into the tiny living room, and Inés gestures toward the couch.

"By the way, who were you talking to upstairs?" asks Inés, lighting a cigarette.

José settles into the hard chair beside the window. Heat oscillates. He concentrates on the little birds pecking at rice scraps on the pavement. "When?"

"Last night." She uncrosses her legs, as if to stand up.

José shrugs. "No one. Just myself."

Inés does not look amused. "Well, it didn't sound that way from downstairs. You know, I would like my place back soon. This store is my livelihood."

Behind her, Pereira's feet are sticking out from under the Turkish rug.

⸙

The phone rings. "It's for you," Inés says. "Your mother."

He grabs the receiver. "Mami?"

"We are meeting for lunch today. Two o'clock. I will bring the car."

"All right."

"Benny thinks you should train to become an architect."

"Will he be joining us?" Inés is listening in while counting through her cash box. She can't help it, he thinks.

"No, he is at work. But we could visit him later."

"Okay."

"And you will tell me what your intentions are now that you have been here for a month? Or is it longer?"

"Five and a half weeks."

"Yes." His mother pauses.

"I have a job," José lies.

Inés glares. There is another pause. "That's wonderful, Josito. We are very happy to hear this."

We? She and Benny?

"See you at two." The line goes dead.

⸙

José rifles through the remnants of Carlos's research. These days, he can hardly read. Ever since Ushuaia, the soft skin of the *Iliad* has remained closed. One page of Carlos's notes catches his eye: a collage of quotations. A line of ancient Greek poetry, a line from *Ulysses.* A red line, drawn emphatically between them.

José sighs. His father was so productive. Despite increasing pressure from his commissioner, José has yet to complete the requested illustration: a full-size rendition of the effects on the human body of being dropped into salt water from a great height. The body in question has had its fingernails partially removed and is covered in burn marks. It is also malnourished. This unfinished study will form an accompaniment to work displaying the passage of a bullet through the human body. Through sheer force of will, however, the progress of the bullet has been slowed to such an extent that it will take another twelve years before it reaches the victim's heart.

"You are late, José," says Rosa as he climbs into her air-conditioned car. "I have been waiting here for at least twelve minutes. And what is that smell?" She sniffs the air. "Don't tell me you put on aftershave." She starts the car and José is amazed by how quiet it is, smooth and sleek, the grey suede seat covers encasing him in imperceptible vibration as if he is being slowly liquidized.

"It's new." To cover up the meat smell.

"How is the job?"

José is desperate for a cigarette. The car is so clean he hesitates to light up. "It was only temporary."

Rosa's lips tighten, but she doesn't say anything. Luckily it doesn't take them too long to reach the café.

It's one of Rosa's favourites. The dark brown walls and

coloured-glass lamps are the same as ever, as are the inflated prices. "You know my father would never have stood for this," she says, parading through the old-style café as if she had been born into such luxury and not onto a farm in Chubut province where the land was too poor even to yield grass.

"For what?" asks José, straightening his polka-dotted shirt, which once belonged to one of Inés's old boyfriends. She lent it to him on the condition he pay off Señor Marco. The shirt doesn't quite fit, but it has been ironed.

He has just enough in his savings account to satisfy the butcher. After that, he will be destitute.

"For a son at your age..." she gazes into him, "wasting his good education." She plunks herself down at a table then picks up and consults the menu. If he waits long enough, if he takes his medicine, something sweet will ensue.

"Two steaks," orders his mother. "An espresso for me, and a beer for my son." The waiter nods, hurries off.

"You still drink beer, don't you? Just like Carlos. A cold beer on a hot afternoon was his idea of bliss."

"And now you can afford one."

"I am not wealthy, José," snaps Rosa. "Just comfortable. And I'm using my privilege for good. Benny's a good man. He's donated so much to the project." She pauses. "Josito, I'm looking to the future. How else do we get over the past?"

He can barely concentrate. His head is pounding, his hand throbbing. He closes his eyes, and when he opens them, he sees Pereira sitting at a table beside the bar, smoking, as real and as relaxed as any other patron. Pereira nods his head. José looks away.

His mother's eyes are wet but her face is impassive. She unwraps a sugar cube and places it in her coffee, stirs it around with her spoon until it is entirely dissolved. "You might not believe me, but Benny saved my life." Her son does his best not to react. "I met him in a supermarket. I know, it's absurd. We were holding spaghetti. His was plain and mine was whole wheat. I was still angry. I had sent Raúl away for his cowardice, but I wasn't ready to give up." Rosa takes José's chin in her hand and leans toward him. "Never think a day passes when I do not think of Carlos," she whispers fiercely. "But a woman cannot live if she does not have beauty."

She lets go of his chin.

"Benny did not care. He took me dancing. Told me to choose what dress I would like to wear and he would buy it for me. Pale yellow silk. I wore it home and for the next three weeks. I did not want to take it off. He took me back to my apartment and cooked for me."

"He did not tell me the truth when I phoned."

"No. He thought I should be the one to tell you." Rosa looks up. "He wants us to be a family." She pauses. "But I'm not so sure."

The steaks have arrived and are lowered to the table with ceremony.

"Give me some of that," says Pereira, suddenly over José's shoulder, "the flesh of the oppressed."

"Fuck off," mutters José.

His mother flinches. "I do not like it when you use such language. We have noticed this talking to yourself, you know."

"We?" José's mouth is full of meat.

"Benny and I." Rosa puts her cutlery down. "That time you visited. You were muttering, in the washroom. What is this about?"

"I do not want to eat any more, Mami." José pushes his plate away.

"Have some salad. Maybe some bread."

He cuts off a tiny cube of meat, forks it into his mouth. He has been a loyal patriot. He has never told his mother anything about what happened out there. But he's tired now, so tired. It's then he feels something cold press against his temple. His jaw slackens and a piece of half-chewed beef falls onto the table cloth.

"José, your mouth is open."

He retrieves another piece of meat, closes his mouth very carefully, and begins to chew. Pereira's whisky breath in his nostrils. The old poet is holding a twenty-two up against José's head.

"You know, your father was not the greatest revolutionary. He did what he could, but he was careless."

"Careless?" José hardly dares speak. Now is not the time to sneeze.

"Yes." Rosa picks a small bug off her lettuce leaf. "He was sleeping with a woman I only knew as Cristina because he only knew her as Cristina. Everyone in the movement had fake names."

"Where is she?" José feels suddenly desperate for answers. "Do you know her? Is she still alive?"

"Read the report. She is in there. She was also taken. Over a year later. Your father was not responsible."

"I'm sorry."

If he keeps his head still nothing will happen.

"Sorry for what?"

"That Papi cheated on you."

The pistol presses deeper.

"It's okay. I forgive him."

Pereira's finger tightens.

"What about Spain? Wasn't he planning to escape?"

Click. Pereira is cocking the pistol.

Rosa waves her fork, recklessly dangling a purple shred of radicchio. "He embedded information in some of his papers, sent them to our comrades in Europe. Then he found out about the symposium. I told him they would never let him go, but he thought..."

"He thought what?"

The gun barrel is now pressing a circle on José's temple.

"He thought we could all escape and join him there later."

"Even Cristina?"

"No, no, not Cristina."

"But he died."

"Yes."

Pereira pulls the trigger. Closing his eyes, José watches the bullet leave the barrel, and burn its way into the left hemisphere of his brain.

"Let's go. I need to get home."

José stands, staggers, presses a napkin to the side of his head.

"We will get the bill."

His mother takes the long way home. Past the shell of the Athletic Club, the shopping galleries where anonymous ghosts look for themselves in racks of 1970s clothing. While they drive, José feels death move through him, slow as a trial. He does his best to mop up the blood with the pile of white napkins he stole from the café. They pause outside Benny's new project, a condo tower located in Puerto Madero. The building is small, but its promises are big, the signage orange and silver.

"You need a home, José," says Rosa. Mother and son sit together in the car, looking up at the future, which from this perspective is tall and lit from within.

José presses harder. "I don't need a handout. I can find my own way."

Pereira is pacing up and down beside the car. For a moment

José wonders if he intends to kill Rosa, too. But the old man throws the handgun onto the asphalt, and as they leave José hears its crack beneath their wheels.

*

José has Pereira up against the sink in the little bathroom off the front hallway of his mother's apartment. "Why did you kill me?" he hisses.

Pereira grins. "Decisions are not always simple in the afterlife. For now, you should accept my authority." Click.

José slams the bathroom door shut. He returns to the sofa. A second bullet is slicing through his liver. He feels it tease apart the fat and enter the hepatic tissue. He can't keep it together much longer.

"Thank you for lunch. Thank you for the night," he stutters, gathering up his jacket. Inés's lovely jacket, now spattered with blood.

"You are welcome, Josito."

*

There was a silent statement made one weekend, according to Inés. No one shouting, no one gathered, but a square full of neat, clean belongings: shoes, hats, gloves, hammers, typewriters marking the places where the disappeared might have stood. "They appeared overnight, like a garden grown from seeds hidden in the concrete. People just stood there, watching, looking at everything; no one said a word."

Had Rosa seen it? Did she arrive in the early morning and lay down Carlos's slip-on shoes? The belongings were gathered up again after a few hours. But the point had been made.

A retired naval commander has gone public about his involvement in the death flights. Rosa has kept the newspaper article and hands it to José as he leaves.

"We will talk soon," she says softly, running her hands across his face. "You are not well."

He lifts his hand, hoping to place it against her cheek, to give her tired face a place to rest, but his fingernails are black, encrusted with blood. Instead, he pats her shoulder and thinks of a photo they once had of Rosa and her sister, aged about ten and twelve, riding bareback on a horse named Estrella. They were living on the farm at that time, his mother had told him, and eating nothing but rotten corn and potatoes, yet to José their faces seemed especially bright.

IV

Her boy is a colt, all legs and arms. His hands dangle just above his knees. Rosa watches as he opens the fridge and takes out another soda, watches his soft, brown throat as he drinks. He leans against the kitchen wall, one leg up, vital and yet languorous, a boy so taken up with the business of growing, he almost forgets who he is.

"Do you have any homework this evening?"

"No."

"You are lying."

"Okay. Yes," he sighs, his head heavy. "I have a little reading."

"Well, go ahead and read instead of drinking pop until your stomach explodes."

José belches. "When will Papi…"

"Don't ask."

She feels the note that Carlos left her, tucked, tightly folded, between her breasts. She will open it later, in bed, when he does not come home, or when he does come home but sits in the kitchen drinking as if he hasn't already been to the bar.

Thirteen-year-old Josito goes to his room. Later she will stand by the half-open doorway and watch him doodle. Cars. Or horses. He is good at drawing, especially horses. She has told him of the four on the farm in Chubut: two old, one young and one who was stolen at Easter. If she had even one horse, she would ride through the city naked in search of her husband.

Rosa—yes. That's all it says. She has no idea what it means.

Oh, yes, Carlos has told her it's over with Cristina. That it was nothing more than adrenaline, and he no longer works for the resistance anyway. It's all too dangerous. He has told Rosa not to ask because he will not answer. Yet still they tango around each other in the bathroom, one reaching for a toothbrush, another the hair oil, catching glimpses of themselves in the steamy mirror: that bourgeois couple who do not speak, but oh, how they look—his black eyes magnetized by her cleavage, her blue ones glaring at his neck where once she found a love bite. It's like a television soap.

Carlos. Every morning she presses her palms against him and slides them outward, memorizes his face with her fingers, convinced she is the only one who knows him, the only one who could translate every word.

❦

Disappearance of Carlos Mariano Ramírez: File No. 4683

On Oct. 7, 1977 Rosa Rafaela Ramírez returned home early from her job at the Hospital Italiano to find that her apartment on Teodoro García had been broken into and her belongings strewn everywhere. According to the testimony of neighbours that afternoon, around four PM her husband, Carlos Ramírez, a professor of linguistics at the university, had been kidnapped from his study and dragged down the stairs by five or six armed men before being thrown into the trunk of a white Ford Falcon. Shortly thereafter the sun went out in Rosa's eyes and has never been seen since, except during a brief telephone conversation during which the burning star claimed to be trapped in a windowless basement on Paseo Colon at Azopardo, the inhabitants of which were both particle and wave. (Unpublished account.)

⸙

… The overabundance of meaning and reference provides a man with an infinity of openings, of ways in and out of the text… to translate such shifting, open weave is to place the bomb of nonsense into one's mouth and open wide, to place the lips of one's own language over those of Joyce's and explode it also. What remains after such an attempt is nothing more nor less than a semiotic wind-tunnel, an escape route out of the death of the I… — Carlos Ramírez, unpublished ms.

⸙

… and then there is the ghosting of a man by his own intentions, that split which occurs as his body is laid edge to edge with another's and found wanting; that sleight of mind which flips the unseen obscenely to the outside and then gives it a parallel validity, as in Borges's The Watcher: *"The light enters and I remember who I am."* — Ibid.

⸙

Instructions, for a Seeker after Eternity:

Lie on the beach and listen with your skin. Remember, the trees that watch you were once human. The fire is your sister. Take her with you over the dark waters, accompany her in a canoe to visit the bay full of sea urchins. Remember the words of your people, even when they are driven out by disease, for the inlet which leads between mountains will become a highway, down which death will travel. Do not lose its scent. Your soul is insulated with blood and seal fat. You are an infant, on whose fur the snow will thaw.

yagán, kippa, yasala, sapa, anan	man, woman, dog, blood, canoe
hanuha, ahpernih, haoka, palena, afua	moon, star, fog, rain, ash
wahar, wakul, ushipin, saeskin, pusaki	vulva, sky, inlet, heart, fire

Staffordshire, May 7, 1996

Dear José,

I don't know if you will get this letter, and I don't know if you will open it if you receive it. The address you gave me for your mother is perhaps out of date. We only knew each other for a very short time. But I wanted you to know...

Staffordshire, September 12, 1996

Dear José,

I don't know if you will get this letter, and I don't know if you will open it if you receive it. The address you gave me for your mother is perhaps out of date. We only knew each other for a very short time. But I wanted you...

Staffordshire, December 2, 1996

Dear José,

I don't know if you will get this letter, and I don't know if you will open it if you receive it. The address you gave me for your mother is perhaps out of date. We only...

Staffordshire, January 29, 1998

Dear José,

I have been unable to finish. Nevertheless, I am sending these to you.

V

The apartment José takes is small, and the window frames rattle, but the rent is affordable. He's relieved to move out of his mother's place. From the window, he can see: the railroad tracks, the bus station, the villa, the Rio de la Plata and a new twenty-storey hotel and condo complex. The economy is faltering. Rosa says it's an opportunity. José has not told her his new address yet. Instead, he enjoys the feeling of anonymity as he walks the eight blocks to the bookstore on Corrientes, where he sips maté and sorts through second-hand gallery catalogues and dog-eared art books. A tattered 1957 English-language survey of the work of Paul Klee minus the full-colour plates: worthless; a slim 1972 monograph on the theme of war in the work of Xul Solar: worthy. The living on one side, the dead on the other.

Today is Wednesday and he is drinking coffee slowly at the café-bar Lido located near the Congreso, where he always sits on his days off. He likes to imagine he is waiting for his father's old lover, Cristina, who is dead but may yet arrive. She has dirty blond hair and smokes each Bond Street cigarette down to the filter as if its total extinction is a political act. Perhaps she is nervous. Today she will come. She will enter quietly and order a beer before leaving her leather handbag behind on the chair.

She will be twenty-five years old, and José will follow her to the yellow house where they will have sex up against the kitchen wall, then leave separately without having exchanged a word.

While finishing his second espresso, he wonders where Vargas lives, and whether he could track him down, perhaps crucify him in the Plaza de Mayo, that historic gathering place where the invading Spanish tortured unbelievers. He takes up his pencil and sketches an old-fashioned gallows in his open notebook. Then he crosses his chest, scratches his scalp with his right hand, then draws a left-turning spiral with his left, followed by the right-turning one which cancels everything out. These are the acts Pereira commanded he perform, before the man's voice was silenced by little blue pills. They are carefully designed to maintain José's equilibrium. The balance of the true and the false, the real and the dreamt, sewn together in strips and woven through him, fascia and faith. To sever one is surely to endanger the other, but together they hold him upright.

"Everything okay over here?" The waitress looks worried. He must have been speaking out loud. She brings him another small glass of mineral water. He smiles at her but she does not smile back.

❦

At home, he has started drawing on the walls. The peeling white paint creates compelling archipelagos which he has populated with contorted faces. Sometimes these faces talk and ask him what he's doing. They never asked to be born. *I was happy in the silence. I want you to return me to the dark.*

Three months ago, a priest found an abandoned Host at the back of a city cathedral. The Host was covered with blood and flesh, which turned out, after scientific analysis, to be a fresh sample of a human heart. Rosa related the story over the telephone, her voice shaking, and for once he was able to listen.

Miracles do happen, José. I know you don't believe, but people do return from the dead.

His drawings are asking for answers. He does not have any.

"May I join you?" It is not Cristina. Nor is it one of her fellow resistance workers. It is, if José's eyes do not lie, Daniel Malik, renegade genius comrade from his high school biology class. Still so tall and skinny, with the same bushy hair.

"José, my friend!" Daniel makes the peace sign. A nod to their lab-coated rendition of "Across the Universe."

José stands to embrace him.

"You've not forgotten me." Daniel smells as if hasn't showered for months.

"Not at all." José sits down again, feeling a little light-headed. "Well, not quite." He winks.

"The hippie scientists!" Daniel grins and drums his fingers against the glass tabletop. On closer inspection, some things about him have changed. His cheeks are a little sunken and he needs a shave.

"Can I get you a drink?"

"Sure. Yes. Very kind."

They got so sick once on apricot brandy José wasn't sure they could survive. Daniel pulls out his cigarettes. "I heard you were back in the city. The old guy in the bookstore nearly kicked me out for shoplifting but I managed to get the name of this place before I left."

"What did you steal?"

"Nothing. Well, you know, just a little Sartre."

"Still an existentialist?"

"Yes." Daniel takes a long drag. "Let us drink."

José pays for two beers with the last of his grocery money.

Pereira is watching him.

There is a silence filled with thirst. Daniel's glass is already almost empty. José attempts more conversation. "I thought you moved to Corrientes."

"We did." It occurs to José that to entertain this vision could prove a dangerous alliance. "We moved back to live with Bubbe. Mother was getting anxious. She knew big city life was not for me." He plays with his glass.

José recalls Daniel's mother, her home-cooked lunches. How he wished for a while that he could be Jewish too. His own parents were not religious and their skepticism of believers of all kinds was unrestrained.

"I missed you, right up to university chemistry class. Right up to losing my virginity to a quantum physics student. I was writing a comic strip about a couple of bums who accidentally discover a parallel universe..." His words slur together, but José can still make them out.

"You were working on it when I knew you. Except you couldn't draw."

"Still can't. Even worse since the war."

"You were in the war?"

Daniel sticks his fingers in his hair and then shakes his entire head, as if to release butterflies trapped there. A familiar gesture. He grins. Two of his teeth are missing, and he rests his half-smoked cigarette in one of the gaps. "Fun, eh? Got a bullet in my brain."

He laughs, throws his head back.

"Bastard Jew-hating Domingo tried to freeze me to death out there." Daniel picks up José's pencil and puts it down again.

José attempts to sip his beer. His teeth are chattering. Daniel was so bright in school: the teachers couldn't keep up with him. And he was generous. Math came so easily to him he could solve equations while dancing. After he moved away, the whole class's grades went down.

"Where were you hit?"

"Puerto Argentino. Did pretty good until then." Daniel laughs.

"We were both lucky."

"You could say that." Daniel pauses. "So one day I saw this Buddhist chick down at the villa."

"Inés."

"That's her. She told me all about you. In between telling me to shut up because I was ruining her meditation class, she told me I might find you here."

Daniel leans across the table. "Listen. I know your old man was hot stuff. Up to no good. Saving the universe and all that. But you've got to give the man some privacy. Maybe he wouldn't want you poking around in his old haunts."

"He's dead, Daniel. He doesn't care where the fuck I sit." José slams his notebook shut. He feels woozy, disoriented. Glances at the cracked clock. It's three o'clock. His day off is almost over.

Casually, José draws one spiral, and then its opposite. "Where do you want to take me?" He has lost his bearings and has no idea where he is.

The unmarked, nameless streets, the undocumented houses strung with laundry, the ditches running with raw sewage that twist and turn between the highway and the railway line. This lush garden hidden between walls.

Daniel walks with a limp. Nevertheless, he is hurrying, each step ending with a little hop.

"Where are we going?"

"You'll see."

Beside the entrance to a broken-down block of flats there's a makeshift sign: *Church of All Men, Our Lady of the Malvinas.* "I thought you were a Jew," says José.

"I am," says Daniel. "But Roberto doesn't care. Now let's go on in, we're almost late." They go into the dark interior, feel their way down some steps to where a naked lightbulb swings above a wooden table. José can see people moving in the large, low-ceilinged space behind.

"Welcome to my synagogue," says Daniel. "Please forgive all the Christian shit."

The man at the table has grey hair and a patient face. Roberto smiles at Daniel, then at José, tenderly. He looks away.

"Name?"

"José Ramírez."

"Rank?"

"Rank!"

"Yes."

"Okay, fine. Private."

"Welcome, Ramírez. No worries. We are all brothers. Take a seat. We will start soon. No need for formality."

"Okay," says Daniel, reappearing, "let's sit here." The room is full of chairs. It's extremely hot, but there is a breeze through the glassless window.

José begins to sweat. He feels his nerves buzz, his hands throb. The chairs are awful. He glances at Daniel, whose eyes are closed. The room is filling up with men, and their smells fill José's nostrils—alcohol, sweat, coffee, aftershave. Failure. Surely someone will close the doors and exterminate the lot of them. The cool cement floor of the basement will give way to packed earth and then frozen tundra. There is a stench of oil.

"As I said. Ignore the Christian stuff," whispers Daniel.

"We're here for the food."

"Eternal rest grant unto them, O Lord, and let perpetual light shine upon them. May the souls of the faithful departed, through the mercy of God, rest in peace. Our Lady of the Malvinas, grant that we may be free of our suffering, our burdens. Grant that the lands we entrusted unto you may be protected and healed, even though they are under foreign rule and rich with mineral deposits.

"Beloved Mother of the innocent fallen, who watches over our comrades' corpses, frozen in place. May they climb out of their skulls into cloud palaces, the swirling of hawks and condors, see below them salt stained rocks, the conjoined bodies of mating rockhopper penguins, flightless steamer ducks, and below that the bloodstained gauze of fire. Oh, merciful Virgin, grant peace to our comrades who writhe and shudder, who continue to receive new bullets, whose burns still smoulder deep beneath grand shopping boulevards.

"Oh, noble Lady, never mind that we left you alone to grieve, then returned only to beat you and inflict plastic surgery upon you. For you are the repository of all goodness. For you are the ultimate Mother of the Plaza de Mayo. Oh, beloved statue. Hold us as we play checkers and develop hemorrhoids."

An ancient TV has been wheeled in. The snow of a video starting up pixelates its screen. A female newscaster appears, dressed in a power suit from the early 1980s. The footage is a series of clips from news programs recorded over the previous decade.

"… calls for additional medical and legal support for these men have once again been refuted by the military, who claim they have already given adequate support to the neediest of veterans and vigorously deny all claims of abuse…"

"Viva Malvinas!" shouts a man in the back row.

"Shut the fuck up." Daniel yells.

The footage continues. José watches waves of dots swim across the convex screen as if they are tiny fish.

"We go through this every week," whispers Daniel. "He likes to whip us up into a frenzy. But you know, if you want to get active, there's always the office."

"The office?"

José looks around. Thirty or forty men, more or less his own age. Anger wells up, a pressure in the throat, behind the eyes, a tension around his mouth. After the TV is turned off, men raise their hands in turn and Roberto nods, gives them permission to speak.

José lifts his arm. Yet when it's his turn to address the group he just offers his name.

It's warm, too warm. José slips off his jacket, loosens his collar. He begins to feel faint.

"Our suffering has not been forgotten, friends, but it has been ignored. We are the living dead in our own country: the walking reminders of a time others prefer to forget. Yet it is not too late, my friends, to seek justice. The Malvinas are ours!"

A cheer goes up. A dozen men stand and salute.

"Fuck that," yells a tall, thin man in the front row. "Take your tired patriotism elsewhere. It's the military-industrial complex that's against us. We need to rise up, brothers..."

"What a useless pile of narcissists," cuts in a voice from behind José. José turns and thinks he recognizes Miguel, seated in the row behind him. He cranes his neck, but his friend's face is lost, shuffled back into the deck.

José feels around in his pocket for his notebook and pencil. He feels the chair beneath him melt away. He is dragged across cement, limp. He jerks over sidewalks until he is thrown inside a van and the doors slam.

He has always been separate, even before his father disappeared, a lone thing that slinks in and out of others' lives but does not belong to them, and it is not the fault of the war. It is just his nature. He is the mountain lion who needs to remain hidden, an invisible wolf prowling the library stacks. When his father disappeared, he retired to a cave, from which he looks out on the world, its vast networks of dry riverbeds and electrically charged fences. The war has just driven him deeper.

"Do you ever think of dying?" Exhaled like smoke, Jane's question lingers in the air above him. It is an insult.

What is she asking? José does not know how to respond. Instead, he gets up and fetches her a glass of water. "Here. Drink this," he says. And she does. Such a simple solution. For a moment, he feels almost useful.

After she slams the door, he lies awake, listening to the purr of her taxi merge with the hum of the city. He has sent her away. Not with words, but with silence.

If he holds himself completely still, he can hear her breathing. Feel her warmth. Does she remember the first time they kissed? That leap. He wants her to tap—once for yes, twice for no. But of course he is hallucinating. The desires which brought them together have pushed them apart.

When the van stops, it's winter. José lies helpless in the dark, his hands tied behind his back. His shoes are in the church basement, their pale leather insoles darkened by the imprints of his toes.

"Get out." A man in a black balaclava hauls him out of the

van and onto the snow. The van drives off. There is no sound but that made by the bitter winds.

Good God, he has been taken back. His limbs are smooth and glassy. His head immobile, his flesh entirely transparent. He has become ice.

Constellations of light pixelate the fog. A dolphin gull screams. Its wings rush too close. He peers through a rent in the mist. The land around him is empty, no corpses, no ghosts. Only José, the ice man, unable to blink. Not yet dead, still visible, yet not fully alive, that ragged island of warm flesh. The deepest core of his body, the tissue around his heart.

I must return, he thinks.

He hears the voices of two men. "Someone has to die," says one. The voice sounds like his own.

"Which one?" Pereira.

"Whoever is weaker."

"Father or son?"

"Son."

"Hero or coward?"

"Coward."

"Invader or defender?"

"Defender."

José is inside a circular room, in which chairs have been set up around a podium. Mounted on the wall is an old-fashioned telephone. Carlos sits at the back. His shoulders slumped, his eyes weak behind thick, distorting lenses. A man trapped in a tower, who has not slept for weeks; months; years.

Ulises Pereira, by contrast, appears to be thriving. Spherical and pompous in his forest green vest and bow tie, his grey goatee almost as bright as his eyebrows, Pereira, literary critic, is on fire with his own brilliance, his patent-leather brogues pacing back and forth, an overstuffed binder under his arm.

"Rescuer or rescued?"

"Rescuer."

"Animal or human?"

"Human."

"You are wrong," spits out Pereira. "Wrong, wrong: wrong. As I have been telling you. Call yourself a scholar?" He shakes his head. Sweat and spittle fly. He takes out a handkerchief and wipes his forehead. When he speaks again, it's in a whisper. "One must die before we can continue. The one who must die is the one *who is most guilty*. And the one who is least guilty is the one who survives."

"Haven't you been tracking him?" asks Carlos.

"Yes!" exclaims Ulises. "I have him in my sights." He lowers his voice. "He may even be in this room."

"I see him." Carlos's voice shakes.

"You fool," hisses Pereira. "What is it you thought would happen?"

"I don't know," says Carlos. He reaches into his pocket, and unfolds a worn page of typescript, folded into quarters. "The white spaces, here, between paragraphs were once filled with the names and addresses of refugees. As it is, they've vanished."

"You are in me," says Pereira.

"Well, then, I have to kill you."

"Don't be ridiculous." Pereira picks up the telephone receiver. "The ruin of all space," he mutters into it. "Shattered glass and falling masonry."

Carlos reaches into his other pocket, takes out a fountain pen. He uncaps it. It is not a pen, but a scalpel. Carlos places its blade on the crown of his head and begins to cut cleanly down the middle of his face. "Someone has to die," he says.

The right half of his face hangs off his skull. He removes it with a sudden jerk. Pereira shrieks.

José is running. Earth cascades upwards all around him, the air screams. There are Brits inside the farmhouse. He takes out his rifle and aims at one of the windows, men burst out from the door and he fires at them, watches them fall, keeps firing, their bodies bouncing.

He crawls up the ridge, bootless, finds a Brit still alive, his eyes moving inside the darkness of his helmet. He watches him for minutes, takes his rifle out, numb-fingered, shoots the man through the temple. The bullet enters, exits, sprays bone and brain. The eyes still open.

He takes his own father, injects him and bundles him onto an airplane. Strips him naked, observing the bruises. Places his hands behind his father's back, where the wrists are bound, and begins to push.

As the ice melts, José's body begins to hurt. At first, he is only able to make small movements. He crosses himself, scratches his scalp, begins to make the left and then right spirals before his hands fall open. He is back in the meeting.

"José, you are speaking the truth. No one here doubts you."

Can he say it out loud? "I should have been the one who died."

"But you weren't."

José touches his arms. He has not completed the tasks assigned to him by Pereira. He has not finished the work.

"Let me speak," says Daniel. "Most of you know me. I'm Daniel. The Jew with the hole in his head. I escaped from the hospital here. They'd left me there to rot. My friends, I want to ask you a question. How many of us here were hurt by their own officers?"

Two hands go up.

"Thank you. I, too, was punished. And not for being hungry. Not that I wasn't hungry. But for being Jewish. I did not remember for a while."

"Viva Malvinas!" the same voice shouts.

"Viva la verdad," replies Daniel.

Roberto leads the men into the makeshift dining area, which is set up with about thirty folding tables and chairs. Against one wall of the room stand a couple of full-length mirrors, which Roberto explains are a result of the space being shared with an impromptu dance school.

Although the men joke, Roberto is solemn. "Let us bow our heads for a moment and remember our fallen brothers. Let us bless them, wherever they are."

After the prayer, the men fill their plates with pasta cooked over an outdoor stove.

José glances into one of the mirrors. He sees himself among the reflections, a pale man with a scab forming on his forehead. But the reflections are not moving as they ought. The men on the other side are also eating, but not spaghetti, just torn-up loaves of bread. The men on the other side do not laugh or speak. José pushes his chair back.

The dead are eating their own meal.

Who did he kill, and is there a place for them at the table?

"Let them go, José," says Daniel, from behind him. "Leave them. They are hungry too, you know."

José walks up to the mirror and touches its surface: cold. Icy cold. He cannot push through.

VI

"My son, the artist." This is how his mother introduces him these days, no longer embarrassed that he works with the bourgeoisie. Her soft body pressed against his, embracing him, if briefly. She's busy these days. Very busy. Teaching literacy to domestic workers, encouraging hospital cleaners to strike for more pay. The more successful Benny becomes, the more determined Rosa seems to be to redistribute his wealth.

José opens his door one morning to find her standing there with a couple of suitcases and two train tickets.

"Where are you going, Mami?" he asks, hoping she's not inviting him to go with her. He's not an activist, or a public speaker. He works best under cover of darkness. Deep in the recesses of dreams.

"I'm moving back to the farm. Just for the summer."

"You're leaving the city?" José examines her neat, ironed jeans and high-heeled sandals for mud stains.

"Benny and I... need time apart."

"And you want me to come?"

"No. I must go by myself."

After she leaves, he calls Inés. She is the only one who accepts his sadness. Who never tries to change him or offer advice.

They fall into bed. Inés's body is lean and radiates heat. She is restless and driven. He submits to her mouth, her fingers and her hips, rolls over the bed and turns as she pulls him into her. Inés's fury is majestic. Her dark nipples press against him, and then she lifts up, drops her head back. José closes his eyes. When he opens them again, he's slick with their sweat.

Afterwards, he allows her to massage the stubs of his fingers, and to press gently on his palms. Slowly, his fingers are shrinking in on themselves, struggling to reach as far as they used to. Inés insists on stroking them, always up and outward.

It's true; he must not give up. He must try.

❦

A year after his mother leaves the city, José sits at his desk, sips cold coffee and tries to surface. He examines his plans for a Malvinas memorial sculpture: a collection of stepping stones, rocks from each of the provinces, laid across the tundra. Lately he has been exhausted by everything, by the effort it takes to rise, switch on the fan, open the balcony door, and stumble across the cracked linoleum to his bed. This city, with its pervasive aroma of dank river water, car exhaust and rotting fruit. The unnamed rocks still heavy in his chest.

The prospect of returning brings him hope.

His pseudonym arrived in a dream last summer: *La Bomba.* He scrawled it across the wall between a bakery and a market, where he sprayed his first work. It was three in the morning. He had a headlamp. After practicing, he sprayed back over in white, sketched out the blue fox he'd been planning. An Antarctic predator, vanishing into the bakery, leaving behind it a whiff of sea salt and smoke.

"It's your ghost," observed Daniel the following morning.

The insomniac philosopher occasionally joined José from the other side. They had walked all the way from the slums, just to inspect. With Daniel on security—his words—José began walking the city differently, scoping out walls, imagining what could be. Together, they would visit the city's endless monuments: old bronze men sitting upon noble horses; nation-making heroes, victors of war. The black marble plaques in the Plaza San Martín, where the names of the Malvinas dead were solemnly recorded.

"Now where am I?" José traces the names with his nerveless finger.

"You are too dead," says Daniel. "You do not merit a spot."

La Bomba developed a series of motifs: foxes, horses, seabirds. At first, he refused to paint the islands, or make political statements. He didn't want to add to the cacophony. There were already enough slogans and slurs etched into walls. Graffiti wasn't legal, but neither was it penalized. People didn't know what to make of it. Most of the time they were simply too busy to care, the financial crash barely in the rearview mirror.

All José said he wanted, when anyone asked him, was to open up a hole in the city and allow the unexpected to peek through. But politics crept in: blood stains in Malvinas splatter patterns, demands for increased veteran compensation. He didn't sign these. They just showed up.

One day, Daniel disappeared, too.

José does not tell Rosa about Jane, or Barcelona. She never asks: such silence has become necessary. But he sees the clippings tucked inside her jewellery box. Photographs of grandmothers searching for grandchildren, children of their daughters who gave birth in captivity.

Was Cristina pregnant? With Carlos's child?

If she was there would be no way to know. Lately, José has found himself scanning the crowds on the subway and in the shopping streets, half-expecting a gaze to lift up and meet his, the eyes of his twenty-something half-brother. The passing years have snipped holes in the edges of his nightmare and now its poison escapes. Faces of the young appear unbidden in his sketchbooks, their disembodied hands clutching mobile phones.

José closes his eyes. One day he will write to Jane. He will find out why she left. But today it's enough for him to mourn the loss of his soul, that picture of himself, defenceless in the snow as a boy of nineteen. Jane took it with her, into her other life. Whatever it was she was looking for, she never found it, not even after she ran straight into him. The snapshot was not of him, but of someone else, someone inside herself she had yet to meet.

"What separates men and women?" In the studio, José is chipping paint off an old canvas. An abandoned cityscape. Uncovering layers.

"The power to conceive," Inés replies, pulling on her cigarette.

"Not all women can."

"True," she admits. Her face softly wrinkled, her limber body still a girl's. "Or want to. I, myself, am one of these."

"I did not know this." Lilac. Another layer. Pieces of jacaranda.

"No, I'm glad," she insists. Her black eyes ferocious. "Really. Have you seen what men can do to mothers?"

"What do you mean?" A stubborn patch of ultramarine. Beneath the ultramarine, ochre. Inés scares him much of the time.

Her voice rises. "Take away everything. More than a single life. I would not want that."

"My mother thinks I have a half-brother," he says, chipping harder, harder. "But nothing has come of it." The ochre flies sideways. Now there's almost nothing left of the street.

"Really? My God! You tell me nothing!" Inés crushes her half-finished cigarette in some orange peel. Fragrant oils release.

"Carlos. All those years ago. He had a mistress." Such a stupid word. The last layer: gesso.

"My God." Inés reaches for his hand. "Do you think..."

José pulls back. Paint flakes fall off his clothes. He observes what is left.

"Miguel loved you. Did you love him?"

José doesn't answer. He's almost back down to the canvas.

Inés won't give up. She places her hand against José's cheek. "He once saw a woman kidnapped from the street."

Miguel. The curve of his buttocks beneath José's hand. No words, just desire. José hadn't known he could feel it for another man. Perhaps he never will again. But in that moment—breath, then lips meeting in the chill dark, mere days before deployment—he was undone. Terrified, yet certain. Perhaps it was the proximity of battle. Or just a simple truth his body carried.

Are you sure? Miguel whispered. They were outside, in the dark. They had one moment.

José unbuttoned Miguel's fly, placed his hand on the hardness.

"He was a boy of twelve."

Inés's hand, so like her brother's, soft against José's face.

"Alone on the street, out later than he should have been. He hid behind a parked car and watched while they took her—just a teenager in flared pants—picked her up, carried her to their vehicle, and shoved her, barely struggling, into the trunk."

"He never forgot."

"No." José is crying.

"Even at twelve, he thought he was responsible."

"He was not responsible." José's chest has tightened. He wishes Inés would stop, but she persists.

"For years, he kept repeating: *I should have saved her.* Even after the war."

José sobs. The pain is hot, and for a moment he fears he won't survive it. But Inés's hand has not moved. He knows she will wait.

VII

Two small tents, lit from within. A vast field in which José sits alone, wrapped in a brown wool poncho. He closes his eyes, thinks of his father's hands, how often as a young boy he tried to draw them: a pair of spiders, fleshy and arched, their legs too far apart or else too close together. Once in particular (perhaps he was sick in bed) he even had to look away. It was like looking at anything for too long: the familiar detached from itself and swelled until it turned monstrous.

His father's hands, at rest on the cover of a closed book. How quickly they could wake and gesture erratically, snap, clap, slap or take the lid off a jam jar, caress a shoulder, or swipe off a nose and return it in the form of a poked-up thumb. A worker's hands are callused and rough. A writer's stained with ink. His father's hands have dissolved into nothing. Their bones have been picked into pencils. Whose was the last skin they touched, and what did it feel like? Were their wrists shackled? Were their fingernails pulled out? Where are those hands now?

The tussock grass is cool. Damp, tough, recalcitrant. José runs his palms along its leaves. There are nerves in his hands which fire and nerves which lie dormant, and the grass speaks to them all, as does the granular soil. The monument he will make is a stranger, like him, in this land; he will graft it to igneous clumps of loess for the purposes of remembrance, a fragment of history blown loose.

Preparing for this project, he studied geology. The breakdown of the supercontinents into continents and islands. *Even the land beneath us is not static,* he told himself, bending down on hands and knees in Parque Lezama to nose at the red earth like a humble dog. Behind him, Pedro de Mendoza arriving at the Rio de la Plata and christening the city after its fine air. Above him, the flat, sunken outline of a Querandí man, his hands raised in welcome, or despair. Vertigo shook him. Lifting his head, he was not sure what he would see. The great, restless supercontinent of Gondwana, shucking off the triangles of the Americas, uncoiling them, like orange peel, from its back.

In the university library, he found a heavy, cloth-bound volume of black and white photographs: Fuegian people in the early twentieth century, their portraits taken by a European anthropologist. His heart thumped. He recognized a face. *What happened to you?* he asked the man in the picture, but he received no reply, only a chill in his bones.

Peering at a photocopy of a photocopy of Malvinas geology taken from a university textbook he could barely understand, he pulled off his scratched, smeared glasses to examine the scar tissue: an ancient rock formation on the tip of East Falkland, identical to one in South Africa and another on the Argentinian mainland, labelled The Cape Meredith Complex.

Do these rocks ever speak to each other? Vibrate back and forth beneath the South Atlantic about the old times, when they were joined at the hip? *The Cape Meredith Complex.* A form of neurosis? He has read that babies leave traces of themselves in their mothers; perhaps this was the geological equivalent.

We can only move forward, he concluded. *Further and further into chaos and fragmentation.* Bits blown apart that will not rejoin. Staring at his list of provinces, of rocks that would represent the men who died, the project felt futile; an attempt to impose order where there could be none. Bronze, marble, steel: the materials of certainty. What was needed was something more responsive. Basalt, shale, sandstone. Flint. Flesh.

Tomorrow, he will begin to clear the turf, along which he and Inés will lay their 649 rocks. One for each of the fallen, the gaps in between for the living. Miguel will be honoured by a circle of granite; José will not be honoured at all.

Inés, in the other tent, is sorting the stones. Each one, labelled by province, regiment, and rank, has been donated by a family, or a veteran. They are circular and flat, as far as possible, and will form a makeshift path, with no start or destination; a floating path, across the low hill above the cemetery. It's been hard to gain permission to erect it, but at last they have found a landowner willing to let them. The location is not José's first choice, but will do. Islanders do not welcome Argentine interference. Most are polite; all keep their distance. Some speak more freely to Inés.

She emerges from the tent. "Let's go," she says, wiping her hands on her jeans. They get into the borrowed jeep, and José holds on as she drives quickly and confidently down potholed paths until the land opens up. They park on a small gravel pad at the top of a small rise where a large metal shipping container has been placed, alongside a triangular red warning sign: MINES.

The wind whips salt into their faces. Just below, there is a wide stretch of grassy dunes, and below that, a curving beach, where low light catches on the waves. No human has walked here since the war.

"It's a sanctuary," says Inés. "But only until the clearance begins."

José lifts a hand, to shield his eyes. The whole slope before them is dotted with penguins. Motionless, resting against each other, or twitching their heads around gently as if to taste the wind.

"How come they don't trigger the explosives?"

"They are too light. Lighter than children," replies Inés.

That snapshot of a terrified adolescent soldier. Although José looked at it twice, he could barely believe it was of him. Just another body. An animal. Not even human. And yet the image had led Jane to him. Where is she now?

When Pereira finally disappeared, there was relief, followed by an emptiness. A life out in the world, first anonymous, then not. The beginnings of a reputation. Now, José occasionally feels joy. Excitement, enthusiasm, passion. But the nightmares recur, as do the days when he wonders why life chose him, and not Miguel.

Miguel. The wolf. Whose sister lies, dreaming of penguins, beside him.

Unable to rest, José slips back outside. The distant farmhouses of Darwin are still dark. After a brief nightfall, it's almost light, the air cool, and if he closes his eyes he can hear his father's voice again for just one second: *Josito.* He can see his childhood bedroom the way he left it: drawing supplies, paper, pencils, and pages stolen from the atlas; hear the sound of his mother opening the door into the corridor, and of his father coming into their apartment, with his glasses on, home from the university. Carlos, who has only been out for a couple of hours. And yet it has felt like a lifetime.

Tierra del Fuego, 1518

The man is one with his dog. Together, they move slowly upon the seabirds, who are greedy and preoccupied with feeding. A stranded seal pup has worked its way up into the sea grass. Back near the shoreline, their canoe, with its smouldering fire, is anchored in kelp.

Quick, he commands, and raises a blunt rock. Brings it down. After three blows, the pup is dead. Panting, he brings out his shell blade, and slices cleanly through its pelt. Blood-hot, at the edge of the blade, three world-choices linger; thickening drops. In the first, his descendants build dugouts, take their canoes out further, and spread his people's ways across the Atlantic. In the second, nothing changes. In the third, a boat with many sails approaches. Which will fall?

Tierra del Fuego, 1918

The scene is complete. The positions correct. Raising one hand, the photographer commands his subjects to remain still, as previously explained, and to hold their poses. He exposes the glass plate, coated with light-sensitive silver halides, to the light. Upon the dry glass, a latent image of the ceremony begins to settle. The image will be developed, and the fascinating ways of the *kina* at last rendered visible. His fellow Europeans will be able to observe and to learn. A bead of sweat swells on the photographer's forehead.

Initiation. A word the Europeans brought to describe the process by which boys become men. The people are assembled on the shoreline. They must wear the body and face markings of the old ones. The men take up their positions. The women, in dresses and skirts, prepare to show fear. Fear, the photographer has told them, is traditional. *The job of the men, don't you remember, is to scare the womenfolk away.*

Usually the men wear European clothes, but today they must pretend they have never seen cloth. This, too, is what the photographer wants for his picture. It's a gift, he says. A chance to observe their faces from another side.

The southeast wind whistles. *Hold still.* Very still. So very long, in the wind.

NOTES

This is a work of fiction. It does not attempt to present an accurate, objective or balanced account of events, but rather to gesture toward the intricate web of interconnections which underlies any specific historical moment. Unless otherwise noted, all illustrations are by the author. Any errors, factual or moral, are my own.

The epigraphs at the beginning are taken from:

Berger, John. *Bento's Sketchbook.* Pantheon, 2011.

Borges, Jorge Luis. "The Causes." *Selected Poems.* ed. Alexander Coleman. Penguin Classics, 1999.

Darwin, Charles. *The Zoology of the Voyage of the HMS Beagle.* Accessed via darwin-online.org.uk

Quotations from Homer's *Iliad* are adapted from a variety of translations, including:

Mitchell, Stephen (translator). *The Iliad.* Atria Books, 2012.

Powell, Barry B. (translator). *The Iliad.* Oxford University Press, 2014.

Fagles, Robert (translator). *The Iliad.* Penguin Classics, 1998.

The image of the warrah used for Figure 8 is "Antarctic Wolf" by John Gerrard Keulemans, from St. George Mivart's *Dogs, Jackals, Wolves, and Foxes: A Monograph of the Canidae*, published by R. H. Porter, London, 1890.

The quotation from Charles Darwin in Part One, Chapter Seven is excerpted from the naturalist's own journals: Darwin, Charles. *The Voyage of Charles Darwin: His Autobiographical Writings.* ed. Christopher Ralling. BBC, 1978.

The colour photograph of James Joyce referred to in Part Two, Chapter One was taken by Gisèle Freund in 1939 and is in London's National Portrait Gallery collection.

The phrase "paradox at the centre," used in Part Two, Chapter Five, is taken from an art exhibit of the same name viewed at the Museo de Arte Moderno de Buenos Aires (MAMBA) in May 2017.

For more information on the story of Rufina Cambacérès (Figure 9), the "girl who was buried alive in her family vault" in Part Three, Chapter Two, see https://www.atlasobscura.com/places/the-tomb-of-rufina-cambaceres-buenos-aires-argentina

The paragraph about Carlos's disappearance in Part Three, Chapter Four is based on similar accounts published in *Nunca Más (Never Again)*. CONADEP, 1984.

The words in the Yamana/Yagán language listed in Part Three, Chapter Four are taken variously from the Thomas Bridges dictionary, http://archive.org/details/YAMANA-ENGLISHA/page/n5, and the Yagán dictionary for the endangered languages project, http://ids.clld.org/contributions/315

Ulises Pereira's words in Part Three, Chapter Five, "The ruin of all space ... Shattered glass, and falling masonry," are drawn from Stephen Dedalus's words in chapter two of Joyce's *Ulysses*: "I hear the ruin of all space, shattered glass and toppling masonry, and time one livid final flame." Joyce, James. *Ulysses*. Accessed via Project Gutenberg www.gutenberg.org

I also wish to acknowledge the following, from which I have drawn both information and inspiration:

Bridges, E. Lucas. *The Uttermost Part of the Earth.* Hodder & Stoughton, 1951.

Gusinde, Martin. *The Lost Tribes of Tierra del Fuego.* Thames & Hudson, 2015.

Middlebrook, Martin. *Argentine Fight for the Falklands.* Pen & Sword Military, 2009.

McManners, Hugh. *Forgotten Voices of the Falklands.* Ebury Press, 2008.

Parr, Helen. *Our Boys.* Penguin, 2018.

Bespaloff, Rachel & Weil, Simone. *War and the Iliad.* New York Review of Books, 2005.

Feitlowitz, Marguerite. *A Lexicon of Terror: Argentina and the Legacies of Torture.* Oxford World's Classics. 1999.

Nunca Más (Never Again): report published in 1984 by CONADEP (Argentine National Commission on the Disappearance of Persons)

Nouzeilles, Gabriela & Montaldo, Graciela (eds). *The Argentina Reader.* Duke University Press, 2002.

Scarry, Elaine. *The Body in Pain.* Oxford University Press, 1985.

Blessed by Fire (movie). Directed by Tristán Bauer. 2005.

Theatre of War (movie) Directed by Lola Arias. 2018.

The Imperial War Museums' online collections, and Library and Research Room, Imperial War Museums, London.

The *estaqueo* torture which José undergoes at the beginning of the novel is based on oral and written accounts given by numerous Malvinas war veterans. Military documents substantiating these accounts survived the war and were declassified by the Argentinian government in 2015.

A total of 650 Argentinian combatants and 255 British combatants were killed in the conflict. Approximately 450 Argentinian veterans of the conflict have subsequently committed suicide.

ACKNOWLEDGMENTS

This novel was conceived and written on the unceded traditional territories of the Musqueam, Tsleil-Waututh and Squamish First Nations, on which I have resided for thirty years as an uninvited guest.

I would like to acknowledge the Canada Council for the Arts, the British Columbia Arts Council, and Kwantlen Polytechnic University's 0.6% Faculty PD Fund for much-appreciated support during the rather long years of crafting this book.

Deep gratitude toward Monica Kidd and Beth Follett of Pedlar Press for taking a chance on a challenging manuscript, and for providing consummate editorial and production support. Your belief in this project has helped me complete it.

Much appreciation to Emma Allain and Ken Sparling for their patience, intelligence and attention to detail.

Thanks to MotherTongue Publishing, and the judges of the 2015 Great BC Novel Contest, for shortlisting a previous version of the manuscript.

Many people have supported and encouraged me throughout this creative process. Thanks in particular to Kathy Page, for critical feedback and generous encouragement; Lydia Kwa, for companionship and tough love; Susan Leibik, for words, drawings and deep company; Fiona Tinwei Lam and Shannon Cowan for brainstorming and encouragement; Cathleen With for optimism and faith; Aislinn Hunter for accountability via chocolate; Vjeko Sager for excellent, caffeinated drawing instruction; Maria Carbonetti, for context and conversation; Val Speidel for space to write; Amelia Guimarin for photographic wizardry; Olivia Ocana-Quintana for translation services; Valentyn and Ada in Buenos Aires, for forthrightness, tango and hospitality; Graffitimundo, for background on Buenos Aires street art; all those who cannot be named but whose testimony lingers; OWH for most everything, and for bringing me home the copy of Lucas Bridges; and above all, my beloveds, Wayne, Freya and Percy (as close as I will ever get to a warrah), for putting up with me and keeping me grounded. *Los quiero a todos.*

Cathy Stonehouse grew up in the UK and immigrated to Canada in her early twenties. She holds a B.A. in English from The University of Oxford and an M.F.A. in creative writing from The University of British Columbia. She is the author of a collection of short fiction (*Something About the Animal,* Biblioasis, 2011) and two collections of poetry (*Grace Shiver,* Inanna Publications 2011 and *The Words I Know,* Press Gang Publishers 1994). A long-time resident of East Vancouver, she teaches creative writing and interdisciplinary expressive arts at Kwantlen Polytechnic University, and draws comics in her spare time.